GUN-HUNT FOR THE SUNDANCE KID

Nelson Nye

Chivers Press   •   G.K. Hall & Co.
Bath, England   Waterville, Maine USA

This Large Print edition is published by Chivers Press, England, and by G.K. Hall & Co., USA.

Published in 2001 in the U.K. by arrangement with the author c/o Golden West Literary Agency.

Published in 2001 in the U.S. by arrangement with Golden West Literary Agency.

U.K. Hardcover   ISBN 0-7540-4572-2   (Chivers Large Print)
U.K. Softcover   ISBN 0-7540-4573-0   (Camden Large Print)
U.S. Softcover   ISBN 0-7838-9475-9   (Nightingale Series Edition)

The text of this Large Print edition is unabridged.
Other aspects of the book may vary from the original edition.

Set in 16 pt. New Times Roman.

Printed in Great Britain on acid-free paper.

British Library Cataloguing in Publication Data available

Library of Congress Cataloging-in-Publication Data

    Nye, Nelson C. (Nelson Coral), 1907–
      [Once in the saddle]
      Gun-hunt for the Sundance Kid / Nelson Nye.
         p. cm.
      Originally published as: Once in the saddle.
      ISBN 0-7838-9475-9 (lg. print : sc : alk. paper)
      1. Large type books.   I. Title.
    PS3527.Y33 O54 2001
    813'.54—dc21
                                   2001024201

For
Buck Weaver
—a fast hand with horses!

This novel is based on those wild days when lawmen tried to clean up The Cherokee Strip, Oklahoma

CHAPTER ONE

It was rightdown sudden, the way Sam got his light snuffed.

I had my back against a cottonwood twelve foot off when he stepped from the Buckhorn's batwings into the gathered dusk of Perry's unpaved street.

'Crescent—'

The call came from over yonderly, nicely pitched to stop a man.

Sam stopped. He wheeled hard-bitten features for a look across his shoulder. In the light of the Buckhorn's coal-oil lamps I saw the sudden jump of his hand. The sound of its slap on the wood of his gun butt was a miniature explosion.

'Don't do it, Crescent,' the cold voice warned.

But it wasn't in Sam's nature to heed that good advice—nor the frosty glint of the speaker's eye. With a salty curse he dragged his iron. Flame burst whitely from the level of his hip. Two reports fanned upward, flatly slamming the town's wild din. Trebled echoes scraped flimsy walls and tents' dust-covered sheeting.

Another moment Sam hung poised. Then the hinges of his knees broke loose and flopped him forward in a grotesque heap. His

1

hat fell off and rolled. But Sam never moved. He lay there with his curls in the dust, with the flickering torch and lantern light redly lapping at his face.

I felt a little sick.

*   *   *

I expect it was a touch of liver. Back in Texas I'd been called 'plumb cultus' and had frequent preached a sermon over gents dropped by my pistol—just to show, you understand, that nerves and me were not acquainted. Some galoots would've laughed their bellies off if anybody'd told them Ike Stroud was near to puking at the sight of a little blood!

Thought of them guys helped me and I took a squint round.

The man whose shot had measured Sam was puffing the smoke from his gun barrel and looking over the gathered crowd with an eye that was like an auger.

But there wasn't nobody figuring to call him—there wasn't nobody that brash looking on. I saw him presently lift an arm. Saw the rent in his coat Sam's shot had made.

Almighty close old Sam had come to getting him a lawman.

The lawman raised his hard, bright glance. Across Sam's corpse he eyed us coldly. 'Poor fool,' he said. 'Some men never learn. Today a

2

new Oklahoma's been born; an' the time's quick comin' when it'll be a crime to larrup round with a gun strapped on you. Mebbe you gents better think on that.'

I eased away from the tree trunk and snapped the butt of my smoke through the night. I drew a long deep breath, and a fellow beside me did the same. 'Whew!' he said, shaking the cramps from his muscles. 'Sure glad that mustached devil's found chores to take him elsewhere. Gawd's own mercy he didn't serve me same as Crescent!'

I looked him over and grinned a little. I wasn't much impressed. I'd known a right plenty of bright young squirts like him to come booming into the country these days. They all had the same kind of ailing, seemed like; too many paperbacked tales of the Daltons.

I said without much charity, 'You're too small fry for a man like Bill.'

I guessed that would daunsy his swagger.

It didn't. He said with a snort, 'I reckon you ain't knowin' Bill too good.'

I let it pass. I said: 'Wonder what the hell he's up to round here. Thought he was marshalin' Guthrie—'

'Is. This sorry excuse fer a council we got done sent a rider lammin' fer 'im. Scissorbills! Be the ruin o' this camp with their damn marshals 's thick right now a man can't put out his hand 'thout hittin' one! Hell—C'mon! Le's git a drink.'

'Not me,' I said. Not that I couldn't use one, but I wanted to stay on the street for a spell. I had a few things to look into.

I watched the kid pick a careful way around Sam's unmoved body; saw him then put a hand to the half-leaf doors and go shoving his careless way inside. Just another hair-brained kid, I thought, headed for hell by the shortest path.

*   *   *

This was Perry. Perry, Oklahoma—burst to life six hours ago, and already a shack-and-tent city well upwards of fifteen thousand; biggest part of which, I reckoned, would be hunting their dusty blankets after the gruelling dash they'd made for land in this hellbent Cherokee Strip. The morning's sun, *on this very spot*, had smiled on the drowsing village of Wharton, Indian territory—put to sleep each night by the coyotes' tunes; and now you couldn't find standing room, hardly.

This country was making history. Only last year the Dalton boys had been flinging roof thunder all across this range; and since their finish at Coffeyville, Bill Doolin had gotten together a gang that was bidding fair to put bank robbing and plain horse-thievery on a strictly flourishing basis. Other guys, too, was in the swim—gents like that Sundance Kid who'd barged to such prominence in the last thirty days.

Things would have been bad enough, I expect, if the law's star packers had only to contend with jaspers like Doolin and that crazy Kid. But a lesser fry was legion. The country fair crawled with overnight desperadoes—a stripe who stopped folks on the trail, killed men for day wages and knifed gents while their eyes were closed to pay off grudges they daren't pay otherwise. All the tin packers from there to hell couldn't stamp out this meaner breed, and the chances of shoving bars around the organized kings of crime didn't look worth the risk of betting on. This was a turbulent land; lead furrowed every acre and the rivers ran blood red.

The nation's morals had gone a flipflop. The east was cranking out Boss Tweeds and out there in Indian territory we was getting our second wind, so to speak, in the mustering of gun slinging outlaws eager to try any spectacular thing that might set in the shade the reps of the James boys, or the fame of that damned Bill Bonney.

But we had our famous lawmen, too. And chief of these was the man who had just downed Crescent Sam—Bill Tilghman.

Doolin's crowd was holed up at the Horseshoe Ranch in the roughest part of the Injun country. They made quick raids and quicker flights. And fellows not in with them, who could have told the way, were staying awake nights keeping their mouths shut.

As for Sundance Kid—men threw up their hands disgusted. More than half of them believed him a downright fiction. You couldn't rightly blame them, neither, such were the weird, blood-curdling tales that were going the rounds of the cow camps. Hardly a yarn but put some kind of strain on credence. The latest had him at two train sackings in a single night—one just outside St. Charles, Missouri, the other one east of El Paso. Both jobs, you were told, held the unmistakable stamp of Sundance Kid.

But I had no doubt there was such a man. I had been around considerable and had lived a pretty crowded life for a fellow not twenty-three till next grass. I had seen some boisterous country, so ill-famed as a rendezvous for rogues and cut-throats that more than fifty deputy marshals had been eased into them in the last six months.

This town was a regular drum for rumor. Everyone knew Crescent Sam had been a long rider with Doolin's wild bunch—fact is, I'd been cultivating Sam in the very hope he'd get me into it. But he hadn't so far. And now he would not. Still, he'd not done bad while he lasted. He'd done a damned sight better than *I* had! The breed was a heap too thick in this region. New outfits were blossoming every night. There was Doolin's, Picacho's, Bill Towerly's and Starr's, Ed Cantress' gang and a host of others. It was a crying shame one country had to feed so many.

*   *   *

Deciding to abandon my plan, as it concerned Bill Tilghman, I shouldered through the Buckhorn's entrance, tugged a crick in my hat and antigodled round till I got my backbone rubbing a wall. I curled my lip as I looked around; I'd been in plenty of places like this. I knew their ways, their stinks and their women—I knew them too well and I did not like them. Cut to a pattern; there was nothing new or different about it. Six deep, men bellied its crude, plank bar, jostling, swearing, scowling and laughing; doing their best, I made no doubt, to cut the town's dust out of their gizzards whilst they kept a sly eye wangling round for a sucker.

A steeple-hatted band furnished lively tempo. You had to shout to hear yourself think, and the smoky deek was so thick you could cut it.

I watched the milling crowd for a while, looking round, out of caution, for a face that might know me. There were teamsters and freighters, bullwhackers, Chinamen, tall booted cowboys, sooners and sodbusters, with here and there the blue coat of a cavalryman or the bright red shirt of a Cornish miner. There were a good many gamblers and the red checked women in low-cut gowns were thicker than fiddlers around hell's furnace.

There was raw life here and wild blood in plenty. Off yonder beneath a hanging limb I saw the kid I had talked to outside. Charlie Kaintuck, he'd allowed his name was. Right now he was bucking a faro game and the slant of his cheeks told the way of his luck.

I watched the play. The dealer, a mustached fellow in a stovepipe hat, was a pretty shrewd gentleman. Shrewd and smooth—but not so smooth I couldn't tell what he was up to. He was taking Charlie for a reaming. And Charlie was getting wise to him.

Men's reactions to squeezed cards and 'tell' cards—in short, to crooked dealing—have been, most times, a little violent. I could see that young Charlie's were going to be.

I thought some of getting out of there. But the play, when it came, came too sudden. With Charlie's hand blurring down to leather I had no choice. It was back him or lose him like I'd lost Crescent Sam. I was between the witch and the devil, and I did what I thought would most help me.

'Get 'em high!' yapped Charlie thinly, with a boot heel scraping his chair back. He whipped away from the table with his back placed toward a wall. He stood that way, with his spare form tipped, a gun at his thigh.

'There's folks,' he said, 'in this here place that's been neglectin' their religion. Mos' gen'ally I aims t' be ca'ful what breed of ticks I team with, but when I *do* git tangled with a bunch of rimfire sports like this I don't much care which I salivate. So get 'em up an' keep 'em—*an' stan' away from that table!*'

'Hold on—' soothed the Buckhorn's proprietor, clearing his throat kind of nervous-like. 'Ain't no call fer you t' git excited. If you figger there's somethin' wrong with—'

'I'm all through figgerin',' Charlie said. 'Git yo' han's up, the whole blame push of you, 'fore I knock the tin off'n some of them horns.'

He meant it, too; but the bar was sure getting ugly. There were three-four fellows by the bar that were fixing to let their beer-grabbers sag. I said: 'You heard the gent oratin', boys. Take it easy on the turns an' don't go to lovin' no sudden motions. You ladies get your paws up, too—we ain't craving no derringer punctures. Just back on over to them yonder walls an' let your breaths out gentle-like. Elsewise somebody's liable to get hurt.'

Charlie said, 'Keep yo' eye skinned whilst I clean this table.'

I saw a dark-eyed skirt shoving greenbacks into her stocking top. I said, 'Don't fash yourself, lady. All we want is our own. Just rest back easy-like—'

It was then that the dealer took his chance. He shook his sleeve and a gun popped out and I let him have it, plumb center.

9

We backed to the door. When my shoulder brushed its frame Charlie drawled, 'Want to thank you gents. Yo' restraint's been rightdown han'some. Just a word of caution— first ranny puts his cabeza outside will sure git measured fer a shutter. Think on it, gents. Think on it.'

*   *   *

After the glare of those blazing lamps the night outside was black as a coffin. Through the murk I heard Charlie's voice: 'Quick! Git up in this saddle—'

'My horse—'

'Hell with that! Git up an' be quick!'

Oh, well, I thought. Might's well be hung for a horse thief as for croaking that crooked gambler! And right now that crowd wasn't in no mood for arguing.

I stepped up. 'Let's go,' I said, and jerked the bronc's reins loose. I figured nobody'd see me, anyway.

But I was wrong about that.

Light, spilling from the windows of the general store, showed a girl's tense shape and startled features. She wasn't ten feet off when I hit the saddle; and as I whirled the broomtail away from the rack I saw her. Creamy skin and spun-gold hair . . . tall and slim and startled.

Young and sweet as a prairie rose!

CHAPTER TWO

A vague uneasiness made me edgy as we rode through the gusty night. The Buckhorn stick-up was not a thing to rouse much worry in a man of my experience; it was the borrowing of another man's horse that bothered me. It was a hanging crime in this rough country, for in this land a man might go a hundred miles without seeing shack or chimney and his means of travel was considered sacred.

Yet, notwithstanding the unpleasant nature of my reflections, more than half my mind was given over to thought of the girl whose startled face had briefly showed in the light from the general store.

I had no notion who she was, where she came from or what she was doing there in the windy darkness of Perry's street. I only knew that never had I seen a face more lovely or unusual in its youthful charm and freshness. It worried me to think of such a girl in such surroundings.

I thought then of the mission that had brought me into this country. There was no place for a woman in the proposed plans of the colonel—nor in the orders he had given me. I was to get Sundance Kid or some way stop his circulation. An undercover job, as translated by Captain Murphy.

I didn't like undercover work and never had or would, I guessed; but Murphy was my pard. A cutbank fall from an outlaw bronc had parted him from active duty. They tell me Colonel Yoe once said I make good legs for Murphy's brain. All I know is Murphy picks the jobs for me. Nice easy ones. Like this one—catching Sundance Kid.

*　　　*　　　*

I came out of my thinking to see Charlie pulling-in his horse. He held up his hand. We sat and listened.

Faint at first, but with ever increasing nearness, rushed the sound of drumming hoofs. We had stopped on the lip of a deep arroyo and I swung round in my saddle for a squint along the backtrail. 'Sounds like somebody comin',' I said.

We could see the lifting dust of a hard riding outfit. 'Them guys ain't pickin' no posies. Way they're fanchin' after us,' muttered Charlie, 'a fella would think we owed 'em money!'

'Mebbe they think we do,' I said. 'Case of pride, I reckon. I expect they're feelin' rightdown peeved thinkin' anyone'd dast hold their bran' new camp up. There's quite a passle of 'em, Charlie.'

'I'll l'arn 'em,' he said, and pulled his rifle.

We hadn't figured on such quick pursuit; I don't guess we had really expected any. But the idea of action suited both of us. Fighting can be like a medicine. It can make you forget a lot of things. It suited me especially, for I saw in a brush with these horse-backers a first class chance to sell Charlie an idea of my abilities.

I got out of the saddle and led my borrowed bronc back of the overhang. I jerked the Winchester from under the stirrup leathers and joined gaunt Charlie behind a manzanita. We squatted there watching the trail.

The pursuit seemed unaware of our halt. They were coming full tilt and, ten minutes later, hove into view about where we'd expected. It was odd, I thought, how a man will ride so unknowing to meet his destiny.

Settling stock to shoulder snugly I squeezed the Winchester's trigger and sent a slug, shrill screaming, over them.

Those bobbing heads jounced out of their rhythm. The startled horses broke their stride, confused and tangled went streaking off in eight directions with Charlie madly firing after them.

'Them fellows wa'n't expectin' no ambush. Fash yourself; they'll be back again.'

And they were. Right pronto.

Even as I spoke a slug struck a rock beside us and Charlie swore like a bee had stung him. The pursuit had quit its horses now and was picking its way through the rubble of rock that dotted the pocket's floor. We could see them down there, skittering along from rock to rock and always working closer to us. The noise was like hell's clatterwheets; shouts and curses and rifle crash, scream and whistle of flying lead.

'Those birds are scared as hell!' I grinned. But Charlie was too damned mad for talk. He was throwing his lead promiscuous. I had thrown a little myself, but all I'd done was bark a guy's knuckles. I wasn't trying to kill those poor fools, bad as I thought some of them might be needing it. But Charlie probably reckoned I was. 'Christ!' he grumbled suddenly. 'Quit wastin' lead! Watch me—I'll show you how to do it.'

I noticed the turquoise ring he wore as he went crawling off into the brush to the left. Of a sudden I heard his rifle bang; and down below a cry of rage wailed up and died in a scream as the man exposed himself. There was sound of a hasty scuttling as Charlie splashed lead off one rock and winged a man crouched behind another.

'That's the way we git squirrels back home,' he called; and I guessed I had better get busy if I aimed to make an impression on him.

But I wasn't to get a chance that night. Those fellows below had got the range and their lead began cutting the brush to pieces; it screamed through the branches. It tore at our clothes, flung grit and rock chips, creating red hell generally. Charlie's oaths were wild as a mule skinner's. Three slugs kicked his hat simultaneously, smashing it down across his ears. 'Jesus Christ!' he suddenly bleated. 'C'mon! let's get to hell outen here!'

I wasn't reluctant. But the tide of battle changed just then, and Charlie was the one that changed it. Fair shaking in his hot-headed rage at finding odds he couldn't whip, he'd jumped to his feet and was crazily crouched in plain sight, swearingly pumping his shots into the rocks below.

With a startled cry a man down there reeled away from his cover, staggered a couple of steps and fell. I saw another in the moon's eerie light suddenly spring from his hiding and, with a strangled sob, lurch forward across the rock that had hid him, his rifle clattering from helpless hands.

Charlie's wicked skill appeared too much for the rest of them to stomach. The whole pack—all that was left of it—took out after their horses, yelling. Like a kid with a rattle, Charlie stood there, cramming fresh loads in his heated rifle. The posse was gone when he'd got it readied.

I said hurriedly, 'Looks like our chance to get out of here. Charlie. We better *get* out, too.' If left to his own ideas I guessed he'd follow those high-tailers clear into town. And that didn't suit my book whatever. I said: 'Them birds'll be back here lookin' for blood, an' I don't have none to spare—not on Tuesdays. Take my advice; it's a wise bird knows when flyin' time's come.'

15

His look didn't hold much enthusiasm. But when he seen me swinging into my saddle he shrugged and climbed into his own.

*   *   *

We rode quite a ways to hunt some place we could fort up at while figuring what we was going to do next. For myself I was banking that Charlie would know some of the owlhoot crews who were working this country. I hadn't forgot for one holy second I was here to scorch the Sundance Kid.

'By grab,' Charlie said while we rested our horses. 'It sure sets sour on my stomach to run from a batch like that 'un. What say we stick around fer a spell. Oughta be easy pickin's here. There's a couple gents I've met up with that could prob'ly put us next to somethin'. D'you know this crowd Sam traveled with?'

'Doolin's bunch?' I shook my head. 'We never been introduced,' I said; and Charlie grinned. It was a boyish grin that made you someway want to grin with him.

'You're a pretty cool one, ain't you—a real double-actin' engine. Don't you feel a little itchy, kind of?'

'What about?'

'Well . . .' He looked at me with his eyes squinched up and finally shrugged. 'Let it ride,' he said. 'These gents I was mentionin' are long riders. Trailin' their ropes with

16

Cantress' bunch.'

'With Cantress?' I said, surprised out of caution. Cantress crew were real hard actors, about the worst in the country next to Doolin's wild bunch. It seemed a heap too good to be true that Charlie should know any of that crowd. Cantress was big potatoes and might well have a line on Sundance—it could be.

Charlie was eyeing me brightly. I did some quick thinking. 'Who's he?' I said. 'Don't seem like I've ever heard him mentioned—'

'You ain't never heard o' *Cantress*? You sure must be a Johnny-come-lately 'f you ain't never heard of Ed Cantress' gang! They jest pulled a big train bust down to Lelietta. Cleared fourteen thousan' jest like guttin' slut. Smart: that's the word for Cantress!'

It did sound kind of important, if a fellow could believe they had got that much. But mostly, I'd found, the stories spread of outlaw hauls was usually some exaggerated. 'Not bad,' I said. 'But this Cantress . . . I got to know somewhat about a man before I go hookin' up with him. What sort of pelican is he? Got any peeves tucked up his sleeve? Slick, is he, or just a killer?'

Charlie grinned. 'He's slicker'n slobbers,' he declared, real eager. 'Course, I ain't never met him, personally; but he's got the whole territory talkin'. They say Bill Doolin's bug-eyed about him; claim he's cuttin' in, on their takin's.' He ran a hand across his smooth face

17

and spat like talk of outlaws bored him. 'I ain't never met him personal, but I've wagged my jaw with one of his men—duck by the name o' Hanley. Fact is,' he said real casual, 'Hanley's been tryin' to sign me up.'

If there'd been any talk of signing up I guessed Charlie was the one had started it. I'd heard of Hair-Trigger Hanley. He was one of your toughest breed. A cold-jawed gent who'd no more think of dropping loose talk than he would of chopping his arm off. A damned cold stick and plumb teetotaller. Never touched a drop; and his draw, they'd said, shamed lightning by comparison.

'Been wantin' to sign you up, eh?'

Charlie nodded. Made haste to shrug like he was a hard-to-get hombre that had every outfit angling for him. It was all pure bull and ten yards wide, but someway I kind of liked him.

I said, 'Whereat's this outfit located?'

'Coupla whoops an' a holler westlike. They call the place Sundance Canyon. What d'you say? Let's drift on over there a spell.'

It looked to me pretty plain he didn't know much about the way these gangs worked. Once in with them most gents didn't do no leaving. But I said, 'Well, we might amble over for a spell; but let's have it understood right now I ain't passin' my word one way or the other.'

'Why, sure,' Charlie said. 'I wouldn't ask *no* man t' join up ag'in' his judgement. Fella could

18

most near tell by yo' look you're a kind of lone-wolf hombre.'

He cleared his throat like a gruff old-timer and fished a bottle out of his pack. 'Take a swig of this t'rant'la juice,' he said, extending it.

I grinned my thanks but shook my head. 'I'm like Hanley when it comes to likker— never use the stuff,' I said; and could have bitten my tongue out pronto.

Charlie was eyeing me in astonishment. Here I'd sold him the yarn I didn't know Cantress, wasn't up on his gang or business. I waited for Charlie to tell me so, to fling the lie right back in my teeth.

But all he said was 'No kiddin'?' He shoved back his hat and scratched a hand through copper hair; and stared dubiously at the bottle. 'I guess mebbe yo're right, at that,' he grunted, and tossed his rotgut over the cliff. 'What's good enough fer you, I expect, is sure good enough fer me.'

CHAPTER THREE

Seemed like for countless hours my horse had followed Charlie's without question, just like I was following Charlie. We were going, he said, to Cantress' camp.

It was enough. What more could a deputy

19

marshal ask than to be taken as prospective recruit right into the enemy's stronghold? I had no plans, nor made least effort to shape any, having learned by past experience that only a fool in this kind of business thinks to map his moves beforehand. Presently Charlie left the trail and I followed him down a shallow wash that opened in the prairie's floor.

Off yonder I presently saw a dust that appeared to boil up from driven horses. Then the floor of the wash dipped down again and the banks closed in our range of vision. But the thought of those horses stayed in my mind. Saddle slickers are early risers, but it didn't seem likely honest cowpokes would be moving a cavvy so far from any viewed headquarters at any such tender hour as this.

I told Charlie about them.

'Stolen, prob'ly,' he said, without turning. 'Some of Cantress' sorry crew, I reckon. Must be gettin' damn close.'

'Won't do us no good to come in with them horses. Might be embarrassin',' I said and slowed down.

Charlie nodded. We pulled up and Charlie knocked the pocket dust out of his mouth harp. 'My pappy used t' claim I was the bes' damn harp blower in Harlan County.'

I suggested he go ahead and blow a few tunes. The more we looked like a pair of fool cowhands the better I was going to like it—till we got into Cantress' camp anyway.

20

'Go on,' I grinned. 'I come from Missouri.'

He didn't need much urging. He chunked the battered reeds of his harp against the palm of his hand a few times, polished its rusty sides on his levis and tongued a few wabbly notes kind of tentative.

He cut loose with *Sweet Fern*—which I was to recognize later as one of his favorites. He wasn't half bad. I found my boot heels swinging the time, and when he got done he says: 'C'mon—sing it.'

So I did. I expect the coyotes was mighty well suited when we run out of wind. I know damn well my throat was!

We'd got to riding again while we was putting the final touches on *Sweet Fern*, and now it looked like the wash was widening. My last look over the cutbank had shown me a land of dimmed-out trails, a jumbled, fantastic pattern of buttes, heat-blanched rock rubble and distant, towering mountains, crossed in the nearer foreground by innumerable ribs and gullies like the face of an old mule skinner.

I sensed a new and singular aspect of this land. Bleak and harsh I had always thought it, but aloof, entirely apart and indifferent to man and his many poses. I began to kind of wonder if a land could ape its denizens, for surely this land's look was mighty like its natives' natures. It was the stamping ground of outlaws and it looked built for cut-throatery. Corruption seemed inherent in each crouching spire and

21

bastion. Such wind as belched its hot breath through these cedars' twisted branches held the reek of death and murder. The rocks and ground were red as blood, what patches you could see through greasewood or through the sharp, straw spikes of cholla. Even the leather of my saddle seemed to creak a lawless anthem.

It was natural in such surroundings to think dark thoughts of violence.

We rounded a sudden bend and Cantress' camp lay sprawled before us. Forty-seven dogs set up a lusty yapping.

*   *   *

Bleached and sand-scoured buildings raised their sun-warped planks along both sides of the horse-tracked dust, and sort of tucked away among them were a score of tents and shacks of board and tar paper that gave this outlaws' rendezvous a kind of boom town flavor.

As I was to discover later, Sundance Canyon, as the place was called, boasted even a general store; you'd swear it was run by the James boys themselves, so far as the price of the things sold went. There also was two or three rooming houses for gents not too particular as to what might be sharing the shakedowns with them; and a number of other establishments purporting to be concessions to man's vanity and needings. These had crudely scrawled on their fronts such gorgeous names as Gangrene Jim's Place, Cutie Crawlings' Forty Rods & Twenty Lashes, the Hide An' Hair, Rabbit Jennie's House, and so forth, to list a few of the more outstanding. Oh, Cantress did the thing up royal.

But a lot of the glitter wasn't gold, as we could tell by the stares that followed us. One gent, with his hand on the door of Rabbit Jennie's, turned clear round to ogle us. And off yonder, three-four hombres hastened up the pace of a bunch of horses they was driving off; and I saw a couple others scowlingly fingering their shooting irons.

A man came out of the general store. He let out a shout that would of waked Van Winkle: *'Hey, you!'*

'Don't pay no mind,' advised Charlie dourly. 'Jes' foller me an' leave me do the paw waggin'.'

I was quite willing.

'Hmmm,' Charlie muttered. 'Gangrene Jim's—reckon that's the place, aw-right.' I kept right close, hoping we might get inside before the fireworks started.

There was a brashness about this Charlie, someway, made a fellow feel kind of proud to know him.

The inside of Gangrene Jim's place was pretty much like its outside—crude. A plank laid across two barrels served as bar and leaning place for the seven-eight customers ranged along it. The wall just opposite was flanked by a clutter of makeshift tables whose unscrubbed tops was playing host to a kind of fly's reunion. A man behind the bar said curtly: 'Lookin' fer somebody, are you?'

'Yeah,' Charlie said, 'Ed Cantress,' and about that time talk petered out, and the hombres lining the bar set down their glasses and ogled us like a batch of Injuns sizing up pot fodder. A tough looking lot, weighed down with hardware; considerably on the serious side. Leastways, I didn't see no smiles getting cracked.

'By grab,' said the drink-wrangler, 'where'n blue hell d'you think you are?'

'Not in hell, that's a cinch,' Charlie drawled, cool as frog legs. 'Hell wouldn't let such a plumb fool in.'

That brought the laughs—quite a flock of guffaws, and a line of red ringed the barkeep's neck and his eyes got mean and glittery looking. 'We got,' he growled, 'a place fer smart guys. "Santo Campo" the greasers call it. It's where we bury mistakes like—'

'The only mistake I kin smell round here is the mistake you'll make if you don't call Cantress.' Charlie looked him over contemptuous, gave the rest of that crew the wink, just like he was being extra special tolerant. 'What d'you reckon Trigger Hanley'll say when I tell him—'

24

'Hanley? Did you say *Hanley*, pilgrim?'

'Ain't nothin' wrong with yo' hearin', is there?'

One of the others said: 'You know Hanley?'

Charlie shrugged. He allowed with a grin, 'That's as may be, pardner. What we want right now is a talk with Cantress. Do we git it or don't we?'

I could feel the goose bumps along my backbone. This Charlie was getting too brash by far.

I was fixing to ease my hands toward leather when the black-browed barman made his mind up. He told one of the loungers from the side of his face: 'Go get 'em!' and to Charlie, right nasty, 'Gawd help you 'f you ain't tellin' 'er straight!'

It was in my mind if Charlie'd been lying, it might be too late for God to get there. But there was nothing for it but to wait and see. A lawman's life is filled with chance, and them as ain't fixed to stand the gaff ain't got no business packing the tin. Deputy U. S. marshals weren't never recruited from the social register. We was supposed to be blood brothers to risk—it was what they was paying us ten cents a mile for.

Still and all, I felt pretty good as I thought again of the colonel's orders, as given me recent at Fort Smith, Arkansas, straight from the lips of my old pal, Murphy. 'It's the Sundance Kid,' he said. 'That's your chore.

25

You're to bring him in or plant him one. The colonel don't care which, nor he won't be too fussy how you go about it. Just so's you do it. And—oh, yes! He wants you to know he'll be powerful obliged if you can find a little time to help Bill Tilghman clean up that section. Tilghman's main job's Doolin's bunch. But the colonel thinks if you two could work together a little you could probably clean up that whole damn country.'

Nice comfortable chore. Like counting ten by fives. Or winning marbles off a diaper-wrapped baby. Kind of chore pal Murphy always gets me—something soft and downright easy.

Sundance and his playmates weren't wanted for much but a little horse stealing, whisky running, highway robbery, arson, murder and two or three other little things I can't think of right now.

'Shucks, Ike. That's a piddlin' task for a galoot of your talents,' Murphy had chuckled.

But it looked like I might put it over on him this time. All I asked was that Charlie's paw was equal to the chore his brass had set. Just let him talk us into this gang and I'd lick this commission in record time, Oh, I was pleased all right, and kind of scared, too, of course; but I'd never felt so sure of anything. And I contend I had some rights in the matter. Things were shaping slick as bear grease. Wasn't I right in the very thick of things? If our luck would hold another ten minutes we would be, I figured, a part of Cantress' gang; and next to Doolin's, his was biggest in this whole wild stretch of country.

I figured I had a right to crow. I'd have bet my shirt Ed Cantress knew who and where the Sundance Kid was. I'd have called any bet you'd have laid, right then, that once in the gang I could bust it up, too. It was a tough assignment the colonel had given me, and here I had it halfway licked—Why, it looked to me like that U. S. marshal's badge I'd been promised was good as pinned on my shirt right then!

Shadows blocked the light from the entrance. The half-leaf doors pushed abruptly in and I found myself face to face with Cantress.

CHAPTER FOUR

There was no mistaking him.

In a bold and arrogant way his smooth-shaved, ruddy face was handsome. His forehead was high and broad. He had well shaped features, and there was about him an air of joviality I was extremely hard put to reconcile with what I had heard of this fellow. The cool gray of his eyes suggested keen intelligence and the blue serge 'store clothes' clinging so snugly to his stocky figure gave him a welcome flavor of poise and gentlemanly breeding.

He was born a leader, fearless, utterly ruthless and intelligent. But these were all things I learned later. Just then my greatest impression was one of amazed surprise. And then I sensed another thing. He had not even noticed Charlie—all his attention was turned on me.

*   *   *

Cantress said to the shaggy man beside him, 'This the fellow you were telling me about?'

The shaggy one looked me over without charity, and grunted. 'No,' he said—'the brick top,' and came limping over to shake young Charlie's hand. You could see the kid was tickled.

'H'are you, Hanley?' he said kind of breathless. 'I've rid in to take you up on that offer—if the lay here suits my pardner. Step up an' shake his dew-claw.'

The fellow gave me another look; I saw no friendliness in it. This was Hair-Trigger Hanley, a real gun-notching Texan on which— to quote tradition—you could 'smell the powder smoke.'

He packed a Walker colt in a brass-studded holster swung at his groin, and looked to me like a gone-to-seed has-been in spite of his whopping rep—that is, until I got a good look at his face. After that I was some inclined to suspend judgment.

Grins quirked the lean, bronzed faces round me when Hanley, without so much as a nod, turned and said through his whiskers to Cantress, 'That button, seh, will make us a hand. Charlie Kaintuck, his handle is.'

He paused, then looking over to me said, 'We got no place fo' the otheh one, rightly.'

It wasn't so much what he said as his tone. It was like he had called me a jayhawker. A heat crept up my neck but I managed to keep my lip shut. I was glad I did when I saw Charlie's face. He looked like someone had disparaged his judgment. He cleared his throat two or three times and blurted: 'They ain't nobody goin' to sign me on without they sign up Ike, here, with me.'

The kid had hung his sign on it proper.

It looked like Cantress thought so, too. There was a whimsical humor in the slant of his cheeks. He said abruptly, 'I guess that settles it.'

Hanley wheeled his ponderous body. He eyed me sideways without much favor. I could see by his eyes he wasn't going to forget me.

'This outfit, seh,' he told Charlie sourly, 'is gea'ed t' jest so many—no mo'. Takin' you in plumb fills the quoteh.'

But Cantress, speaking up, said easily, 'We needn't play it that close, Trigger. Another

29

man more or less won't make much difference. What say—shall we take a vote on it?'

Hanley stood in a tightening silence with a warped kind of scowl on his whiskered face. He made out to shrug, like he was washing his hands of the whole damn business. 'Come we'eh takin' on ary one extry,' he mentioned, 'the' ort t' be some kinda extry reason fo' it.' He paused to spit. Slewed a walrus hand through his whiskers. 'You know anythin' good about this heah fella?'

He gave them all a look at his eye, like the question was general and not shoved plain at Cantress. But I could see some things as quick as next; and I saw right then there was something going on here that Hoyle hadn't heard about. I reckoned it wasn't just me that was in Hanley's craw. It looked like he wasn't wanting no new names on the roster but Charlie's.

I got it then.

The barroom was spiked with antagonism never quite reaching the surface. In the wink of an eye I saw Hanley's object. The gang was divided—not open-like, of course, but split just the same. Cantress was boss, but it was Hanley's aim to be. He had brought in Charlie to strengthen his hand.

It looked to me like Cantress figured it same as I did. But he wasn't undertaking to raise no stink—not so long as he could get me for counterweight.

I allowed my hunch was a pretty good one. It explained so well Cantress' show of geniality; was the obvious answer to Hanley's antagonism. I began to feel pretty good about it. Politics and rivalries was something I could work on.

Cantress said, to me, 'What handle are you packing these days?'

I was searching my mind to dream up a good one when, quick as a wink, Charlie said: 'Mostly he works by the name o' Ike—"One-Shot" Ike they call him in Arkansas.'

'One-Shot, eh?' I saw Cantress show a lean smile to Hanley. 'We could use another good pistol expert. Don't you reckon, Trigger, we could stretch a point and crowd Ike in . . . for a while anyway?'

I could see well enough Hanley didn't cotton to it.

And then some other guy opened his trap. 'Let's put it to the vote—' He stopped right there with his eye on Hanley.

Hanley roughed up his tangle of whiskers. 'On'y thing I'd say is let 'im prove it. 'F he's sech a good shot le's see 'im demonstrate. Put up a mark an' le's observe his talent. Names is cheap, seh, but it takes hard money to pu'chase good likker.'

'Suits me,' I said. Then my glance crossed Hanley's and I got a jolt. By the look of his face he was recalling something.

I didn't like the way he stood. Nor the shade

31

of his eyes—nor where his hands was.

And then it came to me.

Him and me had met before. In the Organ country of southwestern New Mexico. That time the Lee-Good war had been on. He'd been wearing a brass collar round his neck and some irate cowmen were getting fixed to tighten it.

CHAPTER FIVE

I began to feel cold down around my belly.

It was like a draft was blowing through me. But that was crazy—I wasn't shot, yet. Just the same my head felt funny. Kind of big and empty; light as yeast bread.

I knew Ed Cantress had turned and was eyeing me, but all I could see was Hanley's eyes. He knew, all right. He hadn't forgot none. I wondered which way Hanley figured to jump.

Cantress said, 'How good is he, Charlie?' And Charlie said, 'They ain't none better.'

Cantress was eyeing my half-breed holster— which is what we called the slash-bottomed kind. I had my reasons for preferring that kind. It let you shoot without drawing your pistol. Just a flick of the hand set your hardware roaring. There had been occasions when I'd been glad of it.

32

'Well!' said Cantress, a little impatient. 'What kind of deal are you cooking up, Trigger?'

Hanley made out like he was deep in his think-box. I knew one thing. He would see that I got my chips cashed if there was any way he could work it.

'If we air goin' to take this Ike fella on it ort t' be account of he's got extry talent. I suggest, seh, he shoot again' ouah friend Bronc Andrade.'

There was a handful of growls. Six or eight guys nodded. I reckoned this Andrade was a right-tail whizzer with red striped wheels.

Then I heard Cantress speaking. 'That agreeable to you?' He was making his talk at a long-geared hombre lounged against the wall. Long Gear nodded.

He said, 'I'm willin'. But there ain't much sense to it.'

Hanley said, 'Show 'im what real shootin' is, Bronc.'

I didn't say anything. But I made up my mind to keep an eye out for Hanley. It was quite in the cards he might figure to pot me—accidental, of course—while my attention was glued to this slapper, Bronc Andrade.

While Andrade was getting himself undraped from the wall I got out the makings and rolled me a smoke.

Andrade swaggered out to the street, the rest of us following. I made sure Mister Hanley left in front of me.

The news had sure got around fast. Guys come a-running from every direction. And by Andrade's look it didn't rile him none. Looked like he figured this was going to be duck soup.

'Well,' he allowed, 'you're goin' to see some shootin'. Ain't no gas about *my* talents. Skin your eyes now, gents, an' watch this close.'

He picked up a bottle, tossed it high in the air. While it still slogged skyward he whipped out his hardware and let go two shots. The first shot missed, but the second one did it. Down came the bottle in a shower of glass.

I scratched a match and lit my smoke. 'Right cute,' I said. 'Got any more up your sleeve?'

He picked up a can, chunked it over to a burly, red-faced fellow and replaced the empty shells in his six-gun. 'Let 'er go, Benson!'

The burly Benson heaved the can. Twirling, it climbed like a flash of silver.

I heard the explosion of Andrade's gun. The climbing can jumped like a dog-scared rabbit.

Andrade grinned and emptied his gun. You could see each one of the four shots strike it. They drove that can damn near out of sight. When it fell there was a kind of expectant hush while one of the owlhooters went and fetched it. I give the Bronc credit. It was damn good shooting. There was just one big jagged hole in the can.

Andrade eyed me and grinned. His laugh

34

and his voice was low, exultant. 'Hop to it, bucko!'

I ground the burnt match into my palm, and careless-like, snapped away my smoke. My gun blew it into atoms before it could touch the ground.

The echoes of that one shot dimmed; when they had completely faded the street was silent as the hush of death.

Cantress chuckled. He looked at Hanley. 'Pretty fair, eh, Trigger?'

Hanley grunted.

'You're good enough for me,' Cantress said, but the shaggy Texan didn't allow to be convinced. He said: 'Let's see if you can match this, seh,' and crooked his finger at a fellow with glasses. 'Take this heah ace o' spades, Tulare, an' fix it up on them bushes yonder. When you air ready, count ten an' git outen my way. I'm goin' to whi'l me aroun' an' cut thet centeh plumb out.'

Tulare reached the count of ten. I saw the blur of the Texan's body, saw a streak of orange flame tear out of it.

Tulare came fetching the card back. Hanley had done what he'd claimed he would do. He'd cut the center of the card out completely.

He looked at me with a vindictive smile. 'Do you reckon, seh, you kin beat thet shootin'?'

I didn't, no. I was pretty sure I couldn't. But I figured Cantress was going to see I got into this gang anyhow. And I was beginning to kind of lose hold of my temper. So I told Mister Hanley with considerable insolence to hang up another ace—on a tree, so it would stay there—and with just three shots I would cut *every* pip out.

Not that I figured I could do it, mind you, but just to wipe that smirk off his face.

There was a lot of sneering, and even gaunt Charlie didn't look to believe it. But when Tulare had got the new card fixed proper I took out my pistol and let fly three shots without even pausing.

I heard their gasps. I felt like gasping myself for I *actually* did it!

Somebody whooped and I heard Bronc Andrade's teeth snap shut.

Even then I didn't rightly see what luck had done for me—didn't see the trap luck had stepped me into.

Not till I saw Trigger Hanley's eyes did the hard, cold truth suddenly up and slap me. That day in the Organs when I'd first seen Hanley some loose-mouthed fool had loudly dubbed me the slickest shot on the southwest border.

And Hanley had remembered that.

He had staged this shooting to make sure he was right.

I held my breath to hear him beller.

*   *   *

The letdown was worse than the expectation.

36

That damned old Texan never opened his mouth. Then Cantress was by me, slapping my shoulder, and Cantress' cold, brisk voice said cordial, 'Go tell the cook you're eating here regular,' and the crowd broke up and drifted off, and Charlie and me took a whirl at gambling in a two-by-four joint called the Golden Nugget.

But Hanley's look had kind of damped my spirit, and I was jumpy as a rabbit all the rest of the evening. To save my hide I couldn't reckon what Hanley hoped to gain by keeping his mouth shut. The natural thing for him to have done would have been to expose me then and there. But he hadn't. It looked like he figured to do his own scalp lifting; and there wasn't nobody going to pass any handbills to tell me when I had better duck!

It was a cinch if Hanley recognized me he was bound to suspect I was some kind of lawman since I'd been with the crowd that had figured to hang him. One thing, for certain, it was no love for me that was keeping his mouth shut.

There were women in this hideout, I'd found—creatures, at least, doing service for women; most of them tub fat or slatternly harridans. There was one girl however, by the talk I had heard, whose succulent charms had not yet been sampled. Blanche, she was called, but I wasn't much interested. I had Trigger Hanley too much in mind, and the thought of my orders from Colonel Yoe about Sundance and these other stem-winders. Time enough for females when I got Yoe's chores done and gained my promotion.

But thinking of women brought to mind the face of the girl I had seen at Perry. I wondered about that girl without figuring to—who she was, what had brought her so young to this raw frontier. She was not of the calling—I'd have bet on that. Perhaps she'd come with her father; some bullwhacker, probably, or pinch-penny trader.

I stood by the wall of Crazy Lil's place with my eardrums filled with the clack of glasses and observed how the camp's night life had blossomed. There was boisterous talk on every hand, shouts and curses and bursts of laughter all tangled up with the whine of fiddles.

I looked around beneath the brim of my hat. Except for the scattered pools of light directly fronting the various dives, the place was shrouded in a loamy blackness. The maw of night engulfed the canyon. Shadows so dark as to almost have substance crouched at the very edge of light. The dim, sickly gleam of a coal oil lamp marked the distant site of Cantress' cabin.

Be a good time, I thought, to slip over and listen. I might learn nothing, or I might learn a lot. Be a risky stunt. But the possibility of maybe getting a line on Sundance finally decided me.

I put on an act to show I was restless. I took a pasear around, drifting plenty aimless but gradually getting into deeper darkness, working steadily away from the lights. Antigodling around, it was my idea to come up to the cabin from its opposite side.

A damnfool stunt. I admit it fairly. I expect the heat had fried my brains.

*   *   *

Cantress' cabin loomed before me. No sound, no fugitive gleam came out of it. It was still and black as a stack of stovelids.

With my breath held I circled slowly.

Faint cracks of light marked a blanket-hung window.

I crept closer, softly stalking with the care of a cat. My boots were off—tucked under my arm. My spurs couldn't rattle, they were jammed in my pocket. Bit by cautious bit I worked nearer. The loudest sound was the thump of my heart.

I came against the cabin wall, muscles tight and pulses pounding.

Of a sudden I jerked my head—stopped tautly. I'd of sworn I'd caught the snap of a twig. I stood rooted, listening, shoulders stiff, crouched low, but without reward. A thousand eyes seemed to balefully watch me from the breathless dark.

Strange what fancies a man conjours such

39

times. I could almost make intelligible the furtive whisperings my mind roused up to complement the pictures I was building of Cantress and his brass-collared cronies with their heads bent close above a table. But actually, as I finally realized, there was no sound at all, save what came drifting from the carousing camp. Neither cricket chirp nor night bird call disturbed the hush that enclosed the cabin.

It was uncommonly queer, I thought to myself. For unless the place were filled with dead men, it seemed like I'd ought to be hearing *something*.

The minutes crawled.

I became obsessed with desire to look into the place, to pierce the mystery behind that shrouded window. I felt certain there was doings going on in there that old Stroud's son would better be aware of. I wouldn't stomach the notion of further waiting. My job in this country was to catch Sundance—to clean the owlhoot breed up proper.

I started for that blanket-hung window. I paused close by it and careful-like set my boots on the ground. It was then I realized the window was open. I touched the folds of the shrouding blanket and thought of the things I was going to learn.

I took a look behind me.

Nothing showed.

It was now or never. I drew my gun with my

left hand, softly. With my right I grasped a fold of the blanket and breathlessly moved it a bit to one side. Cantress' back was just before me. He was bending over a table, writing—I could hear the querulous scratch of his pen.

Except for him the place was empty.

I felt like a fool.

All this caution, care and creeping just to find him posting his diary! I tell you, by grab, I felt plain cheated!

I snatched my hand from the blanket bitterly, moved off a bit and jerked my boots on. I didn't much care if he heard me or not. For two cents, then, I'd shoot up the camp! All my antigodling for nothing!

I went plowing off through the clinging shadows, striding reckless through the hour's thick gloom. When common sense grabbed hold again I found myself on a brush-cluttered trail that, downward sloping, crept snail-like north. It led me through scrub oak and elder whose vague glimpsed maze of foliaged branches looked to have night trapped, congealed and curdled; to have hung night out, like fruit, in clusters.

There was no moon. But the yonder, scudding clouds showed rifts and ragged edges trimmed with silver that held sly promise of the white god's coming; and a lifted wind was clacking its way through the dusty oak leaves.

I went tramping on, bleak-eyed and bitter. I had no business this way prowling. A man with

41

sense would of hugged the camp. But some dark sprite seemed to have its hold of me. It might be Hanley's look—

I stopped dead still in my tracks, eyes staring.

My prowl had blundered me into a clearing—not into it, really; not strictly speaking. I had stopped just in time in the brush at its edge.

With reason.

The laggard moon had chosen that moment to come bursting free of its ragged cloud. Its ghostly gleam illumined the clearing like something glimpsed at a witches' sabbath. It showed me the shapes of two still men not ten feet off, paused oddly, silent. One tall, strong knit; the other slender. The tall man's face was toward me.

Cantress!

How he'd gotten there was beyond my guessing. But you could tell by his look he supposed this private.

I could hear his voice, low pitched and urgent; held a deal too soft for me to catch his meaning. The other guy—the slim young buck—didn't seem to be opening his jaw at all.

It come over me sudden this might be Sundance.

It could be.

Longer I crouched there hearing their mutter the surer I got that it damn well was. I like to burst my eardrums listening and never caught so much as a word.

I couldn't get closer. Couldn't even try—without warning them of company.

But I reckon right soon I'd of risked it anyway, except that just then Cantress quit his talking. I saw him step toward Sundance quick-like. Sundance backed, his voice sharp, protesting.

Cantress growled, 'What's the harm? Can't a man—' and like that, still talking, suddenly leaped for him.

If he'd tried that with me I'd of took my gun to him.

But it seemed like the Kid had plain lost his head. He tried to duck. I saw Cantress grab him. Instead of using his fists the Kid tried to squirm clear.

Seemed like Cantress, too, was acting damn chancey. Seemed like he was trying to hug Sundance you'd of swore, by grab, he was trying to *kiss* him!

And he was!

It comes to me sudden it wasn't Sundance. In Cantress' grip the slim kid was bent backwards. His hat come off and a mop of gold hair fell down round his shoulders. I heard Cantress' laugh.

Then I saw the kid's face.

You could have shot me dead and I'd never of known it. That slim young guy wasn't no fellow at all—it was the girl I'd seen last night in Perry!

CHAPTER SIX

I gaped like a fool.

I got hot and cold. I shook like an aspen.

My eyes felt like they would pop from my head. I had my gun half out, red fog in my eyes, when some measure of horse sense finally checked me. I left loose of my pistol. If them two had been lovers she wouldn't be fighting him.

But for what other reason would she meet him like this? Why else would a sweet girl like her be out in the brush with a guy like Cantress? She belonged in Perry.

It was plain enough she had come here to meet him. I was not going to doubt what I'd heard with my ears. They'd been talking. So she knew him. Had he used some hold to bring her here—some foul threat? Some piece of trickery? It would be quite in keeping with a man like Cantress. He had gotten her here—had meant to make the most of it.

You'll say it was nothing to me; and you're right—it wasn't. But my blood ran hot and anger—black rage—was ripping my guard away. Wild horses couldn't have held me there longer. I was madly starting to rush for Cantress when I saw, just in time, that he let her loose. Sobbing and stumbling she was gone toward her horse.

I pulled up sharp, my gun held ready to blast him if he dared take after her. But such, evidently, was not his intention. I saw her mount and ride off.

It came to me then what a ninny I'd been—how close I had come to ruining everything. And all for a woman. Just a kid of a girl I didn't even know! It was time Ike Stroud took account of himself. Time, by God, he got that dame out of mind! I resolved to do it. There were plenty of women, but marshal's jobs . . .

What it was I don't know, but something startled me. I knew, of a sudden, there was someone behind me.

Square in the moonglow Hanley stood, crouched and shaggy with his smoky stare gone knowing, malicious. The butt of his pistol made a pale, dull shine that was not two inches from the grip of his hand.

'Go on,' I said. 'Go ahead an' call him!'

The whiskered ape just grinned, like I'd said something funny. He never batted an eye; just stood there and watched me. I'd been sure he would call—I had braced myself for it. That he'd let Cantress go left me rattled and staring.

He was deeper than I'd thought. A whole heap deeper. I wasn't sure I liked it.

'Got a job fo' you, seh,' he mentioned finally. 'Little job of diggin'. Got a hole I'm wantin' dug.'

I thought it pretty plain, by grab, what kind of hole he wanted dug—particular, after I'd

45

heard the dimensions. 'About six by two by two,' he said, and looked me over real satisfied-like.

I didn't cotton to it, none whatever. And the more I dug the worse it got. I quit digging finally and leaned on the shovel. And wiped a sleeve across my forehead. I decided this horseplay had gone far enough. I heaved the shovel over into the brush. If that whiskered buck wanted a grave so bad, he could dig it himself.

I wasn't going to!

Some of the owlhooters had got a fire going, down along towards the edge of town. They was hunkered round it, swapping windies. Seemed like their air gave out about the time I came up. I could feel their looks and they wasn't friendly.

'Oh, hallo,' Benson said. 'Hanley's huntin' you.' I gave him a long, cold look. I said: 'Is he?'

Benson's glance slid away and a darker color crept up his neck wrinkles. He growled that he'd supposed I'd want to know.

I said, 'Supposin' can get to be a damn bad practice.'

Conversation showed a kind of strain and, pretty soon, Charlie, who was back in the shadows, got out his harp and puffed a doleful *Sweet Fern*. He seemed to think a heap of that tune.

I was angling to catch Charlie's eye when

the four-eyed fellow they called Tulare says: 'Reckon Doolin's about set to spring a raid on Perry.'

That brought the rest off their heels in a hurry. 'On Perry!' Charlie gasped. 'Don't he savvy Bill Tilghman is hangin' out there?'

'Hell!' Benson said. 'He ain't no more scared of Tilghman 'n what I'd be of a horned toad, hardly.' And Tulare allowed, 'Course he know's Tilghman's there. Tilghman killed Crescent Sam an' Bill can't allow that to go unnoticed. He's bound to raid Perry. Can't afford not to, now. Folks'll laugh him out of the country else.'

I saw a dark-skinned man nodding his Chihuahua hat. A Mex, he was, who, by his look, had a trace of the moccasin back of him someplace. I'd noticed him before. A black haired fellow with sparkling eyes who wore black clothes—an unusual thing with his kind of hombre because mostly, I'd noticed, Mexicans set a great deal of store by the amount of whang strings and silver they could load themselves down with. This guy was different. He packed two guns in well greased leathers and went by the name of Concho Corva.

He showed his white teeth. 'They're be gather in queeck. You bet!' He twisted his black mustache with a chuckle. 'Thees morning I'm see Beel Dalton lighting a shuck for the Horseshoe ranch. Thees evening, on same trail, I'm see them Bitter Creel an' Charlie Pierce. I'm theenk pretty queeck Beel Doolin try eet.'

We ate breakfast in the cold light of dawn. All around the camp was bustling with activity. The broncs were brought in, all salty and frolicsome, and over by the store I saw the girl Blanche with the spectacled Tulare.

Charlie was feeling his oats this morning. *Sweet Barbara Allen, Little Brown Jug, Ladies' Man* and a host of others rolled off his harp like rain from a duck's back.

I didn't see any sign of Andrade.

I went towards the corral and from the corner of my eye I saw Trigger Hanley. He was coming my way from Cantress' cabin. I kept my eyes on my business. I roped me the long-legged roan I had 'borrowed' and led him out. Hanley come up as I was hoisting my saddle. As I pushed the wind from the roan's humped barrel Hanley cleared his throat. Suggestive like.

I let him clear it. When I'd finished cinching up, he said: 'Wheah you off to?'

I turned then and eyed him. I saw Charlie's shadow. I said, sarcastically: 'Any law against me takin' a ride?'

'Depends some consid'able wheah you figger to take it.' Hanley's stare was dark and watchfully wary. 'Mebbe you was figgerin' goin' t' town—'

'Town!' I said. 'Where do you get that

"town" stuff?'

But the set of Hanley's jaw stayed stubborn. 'Undeh Cantress,' he said, 'I'm runnin' this heah camp.'

'Fine,' I said. 'Run it,' and put a hand to the saddle horn.

Hanley nodded. 'I aim to. I'm goin' t' give you some advice, seh. You're a new man heah an' will do well to abide by the regulations.'

'Are you allowin',' I said, 'to give me orders?'

'First rule of this camp is thet new men *stays in it.*'

'Whose rule is that—yours, or Ed Cantress'?'

A grayness crossed Hanley's whiskered map. But he kept a firm rein on his lifting temper. 'How long,' he said, 'would you figgeh to last was I t' open my mouth—'

I wasn't needing Charlie's wigwags to savvy that in Hanley I was tackling dynamite. I knew mighty well what thin ice I was skating on. But I couldn't afford to let that buck get the jump on me. I said: 'Open your mouth any time you've a mind to. I won't sit on your shirt tail, damn you! I won't fetch or carry for you, either—savvy?'

I could feel gaunt Charlie holding his breath. Come right down to it, I was holding my own. But I was set for action if it was action he wanted.

Evidently it wasn't.

His eyes had the bright flash of steel in their

smoulder and I could see the bunched muscles standing out on his jaw. But he didn't let go. He kept hold of his temper. 'If you ride,' he said finally, 'have someone ride with you.'

If it had been just the ride I might of pulled in my horns. But it wasn't. I had business. And wasn't wanting no company—not even young Charlie, who had just spoke up to say he'd go along with me.

'When I need a nursemaid,' I snarled at Hanley, 'I'll drop you a letter.' Eye to eye we stared then, me and that Texan; and neither one of us gave in an inch. 'I can do my ridin' without no help—'

'You're going to need help if you leave this camp.' The look of his eyes said right plain that he meant it.

But *I* meant it, too. And I meant to go through with it. I'd not get much done if I had to stay put. And if I was going to be dogged every time I rode out, I had might as well pitch in my star and be done with it.

There was, too, a number of other angles I couldn't overlook. The principle, for one thing. There was also Cantress—and maybe, through him, Sundance. It was a plain cinch Cantress would waste no bets on a man who let Hanley kick him around.

I swung into my saddle. 'Sweet dreams,' I said, and rode off and left them.

CHAPTER SEVEN

Indian territory, as us boys in the Service had fine cause to know, was plumb overrun with scoundrels and killers. Four out of every five fellows you'd see was no-good hombres, and the fifth, pretty generally, wasn't to be bragged on. Nor calling the place 'Oklahoma' wasn't doing much to fit it for the women and kids. Every outlaw who could get his legs round a horse come straight as a bat for the 'Land of the Six-Shooter.'

Judge Parker was the law's avenger for twenty-one years in these bad-lands; and he did a ripsnorting good job. What we need is more of his harsh brand of justice today and less of this weak-kneed, puling sympathy. Your average criminal doesn't respect good works, he'll answer to nothing but the lash of fear. Parker told me once: 'I never hanged a single man—the law hung every one of them.' He never hanged an innocent man. Every guy he sentenced had death and hell's fire long overdue him; and those who really knew Judge Parker backed his judgment one hundred percent.

*   *   *

When I outfaced Hanley and started off I

more than half expected he'd throw down on me. That he didn't was due, like as not, more to surprise, or the restraining influence of Charlie alongside of him, than to any nobility of Christian character. He was *hombre malo*— plumb cultus clean through, and must have been near as mad as a drunk squaw. But he didn't shoot and I rode off safe, but I wasn't feeling none set up about it.

It was the middle of the morning when I got to Perry. I rambled round, looking over the sights. The town had sure grown since I'd left it two night ago. And filled—my God, the place was packed! It was like a boom town built over gold with everyone scurrying every which way; it was like a hill of ants fresh kicked.

Tents and shacks of board and tar paper cluttered the place till you couldn't scarce move. More was going up every minute. There were sod huts and even more primitive Indian-type dugouts, and half-dugouts of logs roughly thatched with shakes—though I saw three or four roofed with canvas, and maybe eight or ten more built of bull hides. Coming in, out along by the edge of town, there'd been some fellows busy making adobe bricks, but I didn't see adobe brick houses up yet.

Partway into the town I had to rein my horse quick in between two tents to get out of the way of some guys headed rangeward. Half drunken, they were skallyhooping and yipping.

They come tearing along the road six abreast, catching up walkers and unwary riders all the same as a wind lamming wild through a wheat field. Not that you'd find any wheat fields round Perry. There wasn't nothing round Perry but hell and then more hell.

Just across the road, on the other side, ten hitched broncs tore loose a tie rail and went packing it off leveling tents like a twister. With blasts of rage I saw three-four of the tents' cursing owners dig themselves out and unlimber their six-shooters. I guess they didn't much care if they got horses or humans.

'By jinks!' a fat fellow beside me exploded, 'this goddam town'll be the death o' me yet!'

Blood ran fast in this place. Furious hot and right copious. It was cheaper than victuals and a heap more plentiful.

I kept clear away from the Buckhorn Saloon.

The walks—what streets had any—were so crowded that folks in a hurry was forced to take the road. This might of helped them, but it was no help to traffic.

The rutted roads fair roared with use and the gritty dust hung thick as a curtain; it was a kind of red fog shoved and shouldered with movement. Freight wagons loaded with logs shuddered through it, and great bull trains crawled through its murk like a nightmare filled with bailed buffalo hides bound for Fort Worth. Gamblers, lewd women, shouting

53

cowhands and boomers was underfoot everyplace.

And then, abruptly, I saw her—the golden haired girl I had seen last night in the brush of Sundance Canyon with Cantress. I plumb forgot in my excitement how it come I had gotten my first look at her, or that the place from which I had gotten that look was just catercornered across the road.

All I could think of was that there she was, just yonder on the porch of the general store, watching the creaking hide wagons pass. Stood by a post in the dust and the heat, a-watching them bullwhackers popping their whips.

I kneed the roan over and took off my hat.

'Pardon me, Miss, but . . .'

All the way in to town I had thought of this moment; of what I would say if I chanced to see her. More than a thousand things had been in my mind that had been calculated to help me scrape an acquaintance. But sitting my horse by the steps alongside her I couldn't call one of them things back to mind.

Maybe it was the startled, sudden look she gave me. What I *did* say was about the worst thing I could have. I said, 'That feller . . . that gentleman you was with out to Sundance last night—That was Cantress! The *outlaw*! He ain't no fit man for a girl like you . . .'

It was the look of her eyes that stopped me. And her cheeks—they was white as a wagon sheet.

'What—what do you mean?'

I should of known better; should have known by the queer, warped sound of her voice. But my wits had plumb gone off and left me. I said: 'That man you met in the clearin' last night. That was Cantress! God's blood, girl! He's a blackguard of the foulest stripe—'

'You're mad!' she cried. 'I met nobody last night. I never went near that—'

A man's voice then, gruff and loud and irritable, came demandingly out of the store's open doorway. A paunchy man with unshaved, purple jowls shambled out and stood there glowering down at me. 'What's this feller want?' he said. Then, 'Betsy—' he choked, whirling round on her, 'ain't I told you before not to talk to these tramps?'

Fixing to look like a tramp, and getting called one—and to your face, at that, ain't quite the same thing by a long shot. I reckon I give him a pretty tough look, but before I could unlimber any chin music at him, the girl spoke up to say: 'He's no tramp, Uncle. He's some kind of peace officer. He was asking for Billy Tilghman—'

'Does this store look like a marshal's office? Thinks I keep 'im in my pocket, mebbe! Peace officer! He looks like a peace officer, *he* does!'

'My name,' I said, and stopped right there.

A couple more guys had stopped out behind him. One of them, a good looking fellow in his early thirties, was dressed like a cowhand. The

55

other was a sawed-off runt in black, baggy store clothes, with a goatee and mustache, and a sparkly gold watch chain draped across his silk vest that was big enough—the watch chain, I mean—to have hoisted an anchor. They were both grinning. They had pretty good reason. They knew me.

And I knew them—without pleasure. They were Charlie Pierce and George Newcomb. Six months ago Heck Thomas and me had chased them from hell to breakfast. We'd have bet our shirts they was splitting swag with the Dalton boys, but we never could prove it. I wondered what they were up to here.

'Howdy, Ike,' Pierce said real cordial. 'Long time no see. Where you holin' up at?' And George Newcomb, chuckling, observed, 'We allus figgered you'd be glad to see us, Ike. What you lookin' so down in the mouth for? You ain't mislaid no law wagons have you, Ike?'

They were great guys, as full of hell as a two-year-old stud. They knew damn well Heck and me had been after them. It was plain they knew, too, that we'd pinned nothing onto them. And now, seeing me, they didn't have to rack their brains none putting a name to that law wagon's owner.

I expect, like enough, there's a lot of folks who don't rightly know what a law wagon is. There were no jails in Oklahoma. Most of the marshals out of Fort Smith traveled in style

56

and with companions for company. A deputy marshal, setting out for the Indian country, would be allowed a jail wagon, a chuck wagon and a cavvy of extra horses. A petty star packer, known officially as 'guard,' would help move this caravan and keep his eye on the prisoners. By some kind of fluke of the red tape variety I was not, on this detail, issued any of these things but the jail wagon. It was this—more usually called a 'law' wagon—that I had ditched outside of Perry. Naturally I had done my best to conceal it, but I had been only too well aware that sooner or later somebody would find it. Evidently Pierce and Newcomb had.

And now, seeing me, they had guessed whose it was, and were bent on ribbing me proper. They had sensed right away by the look of me that I wasn't aiming to advertise my connection with Fort Smith. It pleased their sense of humor to advertise it for me, and this they were doing with considerable gusto when I told them angrily to choke off the blat, that I was plumb fed up with star packing. I gave all and sundry to understand that I hadn't been paid for damn near a year, and wasn't going to run off my hocks any more for the law till I was paid. To give the tale additional color I cited the case of the Dalton boys, which they knew it already a heap better than I did: how if the hundreds of dollars the government had owed Bob Dalton in fees, earned as deputy marshal, had been paid, there would probably never have been any Dalton gang. I said the government could take their job and chew it with their tobacco.

I got away from them fellows finally, but I was a long way from sure I'd convinced them. One thing was certain, whether they said anything more about me or not, what they'd already said would mighty quick get around. I would have to move fast or the Cantress gang would have my hide on the fence.

I hoped there was none of them around town now.

My remembery got to working then and I recollected how it had been said last November that the reason Doolin, Newcomb and Pierce had not been cashed in with the Daltons at Coffeyville, was because a few days earlier the Daltons had parted trail with the trio, easing them out of the gang because they were too brash to have around with safety.

And now Doolin had got his own gang, and it was dollars to doughnuts Pierce and Newcomb were in it. It was almighty lucky for me, I thought, I had not tried to join up with Doolin!

*   *   *

I had come into town to tip off Bill Tilghman to the likelihood of a Doolin raid; but it didn't much look like I would get to him now.

Thanks to the golden haired Betsy, booming Perry would have to look out for itself. It would never do now for me to be seen with Bill Tilghman. The girl had called me a peace officer, and Pierce and Newcomb had backed her up. In a matter of hours, I would be a marked man. News of that kind had a habit of spreading, and I'd been packing the tin plenty long enough to know what a sizable proportion of the country's citizens had no use for the law at all. They'd be quick to hamper any pointed-out lawman and indefatigable in obstructing his efforts—until, that is, their own toes got stomped on. They would howl to high heaven when that happened; I had seen them frothing, time without end, and had heard their mouthings about the law's impotence. But that wouldn't stop them from blocking me now.

Be the part of prudence to keep away from Bill Tilghman. To do all what I could to stamp out this distrust. To show by my actions I was done with the law. I began to look round for a means to this end. I tied my horse to a hitch rack and joined the jostling crowds milling round.

This was the street that housed the Buckhorn Saloon where I'd seen Bill Tilghman kill Crescent Sam. It had been, last week, the only road through the drowsy village of Wharton, Indian territory. This had *been* Wharton—that same whistle stop on the A. T. & S. F. which, precious little better than a year before, had been treated to a sample of the Dalton boys' style. They'd taken fourteen thousand from the Texas Express, and not a hand had been raised against them.

The self same place; but now its sound was like the clatter wheels of hell. Gritty red dust hung thick above it. New walks had been built to flank its new streets, walks bulging and groaning with the weight of new people. Fierce turmoil gripped it. Fiddle scrape and whip snap vied with the creak and jolting of wagons that crawled hub to hub through its red confusion. Oaths and raucous shouts of laughter burst from saloons and nearby brothels in gusty, bludgeoning waves of sound; and the wonder was that four days back you could not have scared up twenty white men within ten miles of this howling bedlam.

It was tough luck that girl called me a lawman—ill chance of the most unenviable kind. She couldn't have known it. Couldn't even guess it. She'd been frantic lest her uncle should learn of her escapade. When he'd come busting in on our jaw wagging she had said the first thing she had thought of to quiet him. It wasn't malicious—it was just my tough luck it had happened to be true.

But it wasn't going to make my job any softer. I was to get Sundance and help Bill Tilghman. It was beginning to look like a pretty large chore. And then of a sudden I glanced up and went still.

I was jarred to my boot heels. I had stopped square in front of Bill Tilghman's office!

Sometimes, under stress, a man's mind balks completely. Danger, with others, proves too heady a stimulant. Just a few lucky souls ride cool through a tight place.

It was that way with me.

I felt cold as a well chain. I knew right away what the facts were—the chances. Here was my chance to warn Bill Tilghman. He was in his office; through the open door I could see his long shadow. About ten steps and five minutes would do it.

It would take that long—I had no doubt about that part. I was clad like a ruffian, like a border gunman come north to keep healthy.

Tilghman and me hadn't never met. Before he would act on any word of mine he'd have to know who I was, and a whole lot of other things. He was no damn fool; and a marshal's badge can easy be slipped from one man's shirt to another man's pocket. I'd have to answer some questions.

It was a whole heap likely that someone would see me. Someone connected with the owlhooter breed.

I knew the answer to that. I didn't like it. But this town ought to have warning. And there was my record to think of, and the promotion I'd been promised if I could pull this thing off proper. Also—and more important both ways—there was Nell—Nell

Stroud, my kid sister, who pretended to be happy though she lived her life in a wheel chair and was dependent on my wage.

I hadn't paused but a second. I had known all the time that I'd see Tilghman.

I was onto the walk and crossing it when a man coming down it toward me suddenly, wildly leapt for the road. Wheeling, I saw another guy jump, and three-four more clawing mad for a doorway. And then my glance slammed square into Benson.

His lips was shaped in a wicked snarl.

It was pointblank range and both of us fired.

I didn't wait to see him drop. I took out down an alley like all hell was after me—and by the sound, at least half of hell was. Flying lead screamed past my shoulders as I ducked between two tents' tight canvas and skittered round a far tent's corner and into the open back door of a brothel. I knocked two husky teamsters sprawling and left the dames raising cain in six lingos. I came onto the street and grabbed a horse. I didn't ask whose it was— didn't give a damn. I snatched loose the reins and reached for the horn.

I was making ready to roll my tail when a door banged back and somebody yelled:

'Hop outa that saddle! Quick, by Gawd, or I'll let you have it!'

CHAPTER EIGHT

When I heard that yell I didn't need to look round. I knew right off it was the owner of the horse. I could do two things. I could run or I could argue. I was swinging my heels to spur for the high spots when another voice leached through the brittle pause:

'Just a moment, friend. If it's that bronc you're after, charge yo' bill to Cantress. Charge yo' bill to Cantress or bring yo' fight to me.'

I had braced myself. I damn near fell off the horse when I heard those words. That soft and carelessly earnest drawl could belong to no one but Charlie Kaintuck. And sure enough! The glance I chucked across my shoulder found him lazily lounged by the tie rail, just back of me. His hands were empty, well away from his pistol. His buck teeth showed through the shape of his smile.

*   *   *

A big man stood, half turned, just beside him with a rifle half lifted in his white knuckled hands. The eyes in his flushed, beefy face showed startled; showed startled, uneasy, and just a little bit scared. I reckoned his mind had took Charlie for Cantress.

And then, just beyond him, I saw the Mexican, Concho Corva. There was a odd kind of something in the look Corva gave me. But I hadn't no time to think on it then.

The big rifle packer had backed off a step and was mumbling something under his breath when splintering glass snatched our eyes to the brothel.

The tube of a gun showed its gleam through a window. A lance of bright flame sheared near Charlie. I heard a choked scream as the gun's snout vanished.

I remembered the teamsters. It was them, right enough. A door banged back and I saw the man's partner as a vague, wilting blur through the ear-splitting crash of Charlie's big pistol.

Then Corva's gun roared as Charlie lunged for a saddle. I saw him, tall in the stirrups, gun waving and grinning—saw the crowds on the walks scuttling off like scared rabbits. Then Corva was up on a third stolen horse and we were yipping and spurring, rushing mad through the bedlam; and I was in fine shape to look the part of an outlaw.

I guessed I could talk till doomsday without convincing Bill Tilghman of anything now.

*   *   *

By the look of the night—by the moon's far slanting, it was close to dawn when something woke me. I stayed where I was and collected my thinking. Our return to camp had evoked no comment. I had seen neither Hanley nor Andrade nor Cantress. It had been pretty dark and the fires hadn't helped none. You couldn't rightly tell, but it had been my impression the camp was deserted. There weren't many broncs in the big corral.

The need had been on me for catching some shut-eye, and I picked up my bedroll and went off in the brush.

I'd too much on my mind for sleep to come easy. I kept remembering things. Like the look of that Betsy. Like the lies she had told. Like the rotten damn luck that made some of them true. Not that I blamed her. She couldn't tell her uncle . . . not about Sundance Canyon. Nor about meeting Cantress. No girl could.

But I couldn't help wondering why she had done it. Only thing I could think of was Cantress had made her. But why? And how could he? What hold could he have on a girl so sweet? so young—so unlikely? It must be Old Man O'Daye, her storekeeping uncle, who had got himself caught in Ed Cantress' clutches.

Seemed a heap more likely, anyway. And by threats, by coercion . . . Yes. That was it.

I thought quite a spell about what she had said. About me being a lawman. She couldn't have known that. Nor could she have known me acquainted with Pierce and George Newcomb. Only pure chance had brought those sidewinders into this.

Only one thing could have brought them around here. Profit. Doolin and them had been old saddlemates. Being here proved them members of Bill Doolin's wild bunch.

They would tell him about me.

Yes; they'd do that, certainly. I would have to work fast with this Cantress outfit.

But I'd one fair chance. One thing in my favor. I was warned. And the gang didn't know that Benson had spotted me heading for Bill's office. And that yarn I'd spun about being through with the law was going to sound a heap more real when the word got around about that horse stealing business and our fight with the teamsters in front of that brothel.

I thought of Betsy. Seemed like I spent most of my time thinking of her, a heap too much of it to serve my best interests. She was like to get my name on a bullet if I didn't start tending to business closer.

But I kept on thinking of her. Her hair was a tawny gold, like taffy. But her eyes were what you saw first off, and recollected longest. They was set wide apart under tawny lashes. Blue like mountain lupine . . . strange and deep as pools at twilight, or like a mountain stream at dawn. Her skin was like oleander petals and her mouth was red as goat's blood, almost. I could talk for hours of what she looked like, but you'd have to see her to know her really.

There ain't enough words to properly tell you.

I lay for a long while thinking of her; then I thought of Fort Smith, of old Heck Thomas, of the other marshals—off just now and probably fooling around at Barland's, playing the games and swapping tall ones. Frank Barland's saloon was the favorite lounging place of the Fort Smith star packers when they wasn't on duty.

The last thing I thought of was Betsy O'Daye . . .

And then, of a sudden, I was wide awake.

*   *   *

I couldn't name what it was that woke me. All I know is that I woke up sudden. But, like I said, I didn't move round none.

I lay right still with my ears stretched, listening. Looking round at the camp through the cracks of my eyes; looking round, I mean, so far as I was able.

All I could hear was the wheedle of crickets. Then a low-held voice, not two foot off, said: 'But I'm still the boss. And I'll have my way.'

It was Cantress' voice, kind of choked and husky.

It was Hanley answered. 'The boys won't like it, seh. The's some of them wagglin' theah jaws aw'ready—'

'Then let them wag them.'

'Shore. It's aw'right with me, only—'

'Are you presuming,' Cantress growled, 'to

tell me what I can or can't do? By God, you go too far, Hanley!'

Talk sloughed off. I reckoned they was glaring at each other right earnest.

I was gathering my legs for a dive in the chaparral when Hanley grunts: 'That is fool's talk, seh. No mo' sense to than the talk o' me wantin' t' boss this outfit. Boss!' he snorted. 'We'd last about as long as a late June frost 'f I was t' try *my* hand at bossin' things. Facts is facts an' we got to face 'em. Women an' bizness jest don't mix.'

'What about your campful of harlots? If you'd practice what you—'

'Harlot's is one thing,' Hanley grumbled. 'But gals of Miz' Betsy's class . . . The point is thet she's goin' t' cause trouble—*bad* trouble, ef—'

'If I want her here, I'll have her here.' Cantress' tone was softer than peach fuzz, but I wasn't fooled. And I don't reckon Hanley was, either. It was warning him plain to mind his own business. And to make sure he savvied, Cantress put it to words.

He said, 'If you'd spend more time trying to unravel Sundance, and a sight less sweat on my personal affairs, We'd get along better. It's not Miss Betsy that cuts holes in your pockets!'

'*Aw*-right,' Hanley muttered. 'But no good'll come out of it. You mark my words. You can't have that kind of skirt around this kind of camp an' expect the boys—'

68

'The boys'll get along all right if you'll leave them alone and quit feeding them notions.'

'Aw-right,' said Hanley. 'But remembeh—I wa'ned you.'

And he started off. But swung abruptly round. 'What d'you know about that fella—One-Shot?'

'I know he's a damn good shot,' Cantress said. 'What about him?'

'I 'low it won't hurt none t' squint th'ough his duffle. Got a hunch he's a "packer." Caught him prowling th'ough the brush las' night—'

'The trouble with you,' Cantress said, 'you're letting that shooting-bee muddy your judgment. You can't hand rein a fellow like One-Shot. You got to give him his head. But he's worth it—he's worth six or eight of them young squirts like Charlie. I been watching that fellow. He ain't—'

'Thet kid will make us a real hand, seh,' growled Hanley stubbornly. 'He'll do t' take along—'

But Cantress was tired of Charlie. He said, 'That shifty-footed broad-stripe come tracking in from Doolin's yet?'

Hanley mumbled something but the wind was getting up some and I couldn't catch the hang of it. Then Cantress said, 'Well, keep me posted, and watch your step with One-Shot. Did you get that haul off the paymaster detail—'

'No, by Gawd! I'm goin' t' have his scalp 'f it's the last thing I do. Thet slick-eahed Sundance haided us ag'in an' got away with the whole damned chest! Ev'y last Lincoln-haided coppeh! It has me fightin' my hat, seh, teh figgeh how the rapscallion knows—'

'I can tell you how he knows,' growled Cantress. 'He learns by the same way we learn Doolin's plans—there's a sneaking *spy* in this outfit!'

'I 'low if the's a spy, it's thet One-Shot felleh you're so almighty sot on—'

Cantress' laugh was a low, hoarse rasp. 'You got One-Shot on the brain!' he derided. 'The leak was here before he joined us. This ain't the first time Sundance mulcted us. A lot of good our tip-offs do us—'

'We been oveh thet befo',' Hanley grumbled. 'Did you find thet knife you misplaced yet?'

Cantress swore. 'No—and I don't look to till we lay that damn spy by the heels! The knife's been *stolen*—'

'Ssh!—not s' loud,' Hanley chided. 'No use shoutin' it off the housetops. I'll keep m' eyes peeled fo' it, don't worry. I'm inclined t' think yo' prob'ly right. Sundance's man, like enough, hez got it. Find the knife an' you'll hev the rascal.'

'Speaking of rascals,' mentioned Cantress, 'it strikes me uncommon odd, Hair-Trigger, you and Sundance both limp and are leftpaws.'

70

CHAPTER NINE

Caught my breath in the startled silence that was like a cream turned thick and curdled. The hair at the back of my neck was lifted, and the breeze playing through the cottonwood branches seemed suddenly chill as mountain water.

It was enough to make your spine start crawling.

I looked to see guns throw their muzzle fire.

But no guns spoke. There wasn't no cussing.

That whiskered Texan was cold as a well chain. 'I don't 'low you reely think thet, Ed, or you'd be usin' yo' gun instead of yo' jaw. You an' me hes ouah diff'ences, natchelly; but it's a man's own friends thet he hes t' watch. He don't hev t' guess what his enemies'll do.'

'I don't have to guess what you're going to do,' Cantress said, 'because . . .'

And that was where I lost their talking. They was moving off, their words all tangled with the whacking brush sound. I sat up on my blankets and let out my breath. And then— right then, was when the third voice spoke.

'Well!' said Charlie Kaintuck in my ear. 'Looks like Beautiful Texas ain't no guy t' shout *Boo!* at. Who'd of thunk he'd dare talk back thataway?'

'Charlie,' I said, 'where the hell did you

come from? Don't you—'

'Oh, I jest drapped by, as the birdie said.'

'Well, it's a damn good way to get yourself shot!'

'Didn't you feel me shakin' yuh? I seen them birds was up t' somethin' an' I figgered it might be you'd want t' listen in—thought we might git t' hear yo' funeral arrangements. Hanley's jest come back from a wild goose chase after the Fort Lick payroll. Seems like Sundance had the same idear. Sundance,' he chuckled, 'got there ahead of him. All Hanley got was a empty chest.'

I whistled in the dark—mighty soft, of course; and Charlie, still chuckling, said: 'Hanley's got the idear that you're Sundance. You heard what he said about searchin' yo' war-bag?'

I said, 'I thought he had me pegged for a lawman—'

'That's what he's wantin' Cantress t' think. But I overheard him tellin' Corva—'

'Did you ever see Sundance, Charlie?'

'No—but I've heard plenty fellers tryin' t' describe him. Seems like the gent is a heap onlikely; no two galoots ever sees him the same. The's only two things they'll all swear on: the limp Cantress mentioned, an' the flour sack hood. But I reckon he's lightnin' quick on the trigger or some 'un would of got him a long time ago. Any crook what'll short-deal another crook is jest too precarious a guy to

72

hev round. What'd you make of that O'Daye girl stuff?'

'I dunno, Charlie—prob'ly some skirt he's picked up with in town.' I wasn't keen on talking about Betsy. 'You know these brush-runnin' hardcases. Got a girl in every placita, most of 'em. Bet you got a few hid out yourself.'

'Well—l,' Charlie said, kind of wistful, 'the's a li'l ol' squaw back in Blue Lick Springs what carved two hearts in a coffee tree foah me . . . an' the' was a widder woman onct with ten acres outa Owentown, but . . . What about you, Ike? Don't you go foah the calico?'

'I ain't a ladies' man,' I said. 'Kinda lean towards Hanley when it comes to havin' petticoats traipsin' round a owlhoot camp. Bad medicine, Charlie. Bound t' lead to trouble. You know the old saw.'

'Speakin' of hell,' he said, 'that bulgy wart, Benson, was in town t'day. Leastways, he was *headed* f' town, last squint I had of 'im. Took out after you—I heard Whiskers tellin' him. Didn't y' see 'im noplace?'

'I ain't that lard tub's keeper,' I told him, and prospected round for a safer subject. 'What do you reckon's so important about that knife Cantress lost? I kind of got the idea . . . You know anything about it?'

'I've heard a little talk,' Charlie admitted. 'I heard it's some kinda shinnin' knife. Fancyish, sort of. Got a silver handle shaped like a lizard. Some of the gang's been augurin' about it. Seems t' be some of 'em thinks the handle's holler.'

He set still a few minutes. Then he says, 'Shall we pick up an' drift?'

'Drift? What's the matter? Thought you liked this outfit,' I said, surprised.

'Oh—it's all right, I guess. But it seems kinda slow fer fellas like us.'

'Just speak for yourself, Charlie. Where was you figurin' to swap to?'

'Well—l . . .' He sounded kind of restless. 'The's Doolin's wild bunch . . .'

'Doolin's!' I wished almightily it wasn't so dark. I'd of liked a squint at Charlie's face just then.

'Sure—why not, Ike?' His shoulders came forward. He said, kind of low, kind of trembly with eagerness: 'Betcha, by grab, he'd have us, too! He's layin' pipe right now t' pull a raid on Ingalls—all this Perry talk's jest s' much dust. It's Ingalls they're after! They're mighty near set t' pull it right now!'

'What you smokin' these days, Charlie?'

'Honest t' Gawd—it's the straight goods, Ike. I was settin' in the Buckhorn—'fore I seen you an' Corva. 'Way back in a corner at one of them tables with m' head on m' hands, case one of them bartenders might chance t' remember me. There was a couple of Doolin fellas at a table right back o' me.'

I could guess how Charlie's eyes must be

shining. The Doolin gang was the real cream of outlaws. But I wasn't, at the moment, placing any great stock in Charlie's overheard confidence. It didn't seem likely such hardcase hombres as was in Doolin's wild bunch would get so plumb careless as to talk out in public. No matter how private they might figure they was.

I said: 'What makes you think they was connected with Doolin? They was prob'ly just range tramps. Plenty of fellas makes talk about outlaws—'

'I savvy all that,' Charlie said impatiently. 'You kin take it from me them galoots belonged. They wasn't too fond of the way Bill was runnin' it—an' they wasn't talkin' about Bill Cody! They meant *Doolin*. It was Bill this, an' Bill that, an' Bill says, an' Bill ought. I tell yuh he's goin' to raid Ingalls. I'd bet my pants on it!'

Ingalls was a tough and wide-awake cow town. Being a long ways off from the nearest railroad it was served by stage. But it had a hotel—a damn good one, too. And a big saloon. And three or four stores, a livery stable and a couple dozen houses.

No, I was a long ways from being convinced. What they might get out of the town's saloon didn't look half worth the risk they would take for it.

I said, 'Did you hear what handles these fellas was packin? What'd they call each other.

75

Or didn't they?'

I couldn't quite keep the sarcasm out.

'One fella's name was "Charlie" somethin'-or-other. He called the other guy Bitter Creek.'

'This "Bitter Creek" pelican . . . Did you get a look at him?'

'Only back to. He was a little guy. Short, I mean—sawed-off. One of them full-of-hell hombres. Always gettin' a laff outa somethin'. The other guy was a slick talkin' gent—I don't mean he had tongue oil; he used words like the kind they put in dictionary books.'

I hate to admit it, but Charlie was right. They were Doolin boys, all right. That slick talking article was Charlie Pierce—he was always using high-faluting words. The 'Bitter Creek' fellow was probably George Newcomb.

I remembered that both these, and Doolin, had ridden with the Daltons. And then I remembered Pierce and Newcomb and Bill Doolin hadn't been with the Daltons at Coffeyville. The gang had split with them before the raid. In jail Emmet Dalton had told the authorities that Bob, his brother, had been scared to trust them. He had thought Bill Doolin too wild and unruly.

Newcomb and Pierce had been too credulous, too careless . . .

And now their carelessness had at last caught up with them.

They had tipped Doolin's hand.

76

*　　*　　*

I could feel Charlie's stare. I sensed his restlessness. He was wondering of course what was keeping me silent. I must play this careful. I must disarm him, but cautiously. I must use all my wits, all the craft that was in me.

I said: 'The Doolin gang, Charlie, ain't takin' in amateurs. Oh, I know we're hard boiled—we're as salty as Lot's wife. We make good recruits for a outfit like Cantress'. But the Doolin gang, Charlie, is the last word in stick-ups—they're all crack shots, all killers and bad 'uns. They wouldn't ask for our records. Without we had names they wouldn't even consider us.'

'B-But—' Charlie's 'but' was a gulp of protest.

'It just ain't in the cards. We ain't that well knowed to the owlhoot fraternity. They'd prob'ly figure we was spies and gulch us.'

Charlie took it pretty hard. It was plain he'd been counting heavy on joining them. So dejected, so woebegone, was the sound of his voice I could almost feel sorry for him. He was such a kid. So transparent emotionally. All for a thing, always, or all against it. Nothing halfway about Charlie.

He made it plain he'd counted on me to back him up one hundred percent. He made it equally plain he was disappointed—in me, in

77

my stand, in my damned reputation. 'By Gawd,' he said, 'I like a man's kind of man!'

I shrugged. Kept my mouth shut.

'Hell!' he snorted, and stamped off, disgusted.

CHAPTER TEN

I slept no more after Charlie had left me. I hadn't a notion how I was going to do it but I had to warn Tilghman of Doolin's plans. For months Doolin's crew had lain snug and safe, holed up, at the place called Horseshoe Ranch, which was cleverly hid, tucked away out of sight in the remotest region of the country's wasteland. Now, at last, they were coming out. Not by ones and twos, as had been their habit, but complete, entire, in all their confidence—in a compact body to bring death and destruction to an unwarned town.

It was Doolin's way. Sudden, fierce, surprising forray—an equally sudden, quick-fading vanishment. By such Injun tactics they had swerved for months every lure, trick and trap the deputy marshals had laid.

We had no luck with them. We couldn't seem to catch them and we couldn't trail them. We couldn't bribe anybody to give them away. They appeared immune from the law—contemptuous of it. They grabbed ten thousand from a bank at Pawnee, sixty-seven thousand off a train near Gordon; not to mention a host of lesser crimes, such as horse stealing, cattle rustling, store looting and stage robbery.

They were ripe for the gallows and I meant they should grace it. But there were a good many obstacles sluttering the way.

I was anchored so long as I clove to Cantress. I couldn't join Doolin because of Pierce and Newcomb. Bill Tilghman was plainly the man to handle this. But if I left this camp Hanley'd have me followed—as he had before. Next time that happened I mightn't be so lucky. Whether I was or not, I could hardly ride in and see Tilghman openly. Nor could I figure much chance of seeing him private. I was to become a marked man to the town of Perry.

Even if, by some fluke, I managed to see Bill, the chances was that he wouldn't believe me. If he did believe me he'd be pretty like to figure there was a catch tucked into business someplace. He was bound, I guessed, to see me through the tawny light of my recent actions; and these, thus scanned was like to fall a whole heap short of folks' conceptions of a marshal's conduct.

It just wouldn't do for me to go and see him. Him and me hadn't never met up. I had nothing to prove who I was but a piece of tin any guy could get off a dead man's shirtfront.

Which was where he'd probably figure I got it.

I didn't know much about Bill Tilghman. Just a few odd scraps I'd picked up from Thomas. One thing I recalled Heck saying was that Bill was the one star packer dreaded above all others by the owlhooter breed that infested this country. Heck had also mentioned that he always got his man.

That was all I knew about him, but I'd *heard* a hell's own smear of things.

I had heard, for instance, that he'd come from Kansas with the avowed intention of dying with his boots on. It was said he would follow a trail till hell froze, and skate right after it over the ice. That already—and he was hardly, yet, in the prime of his life—he'd made more arrests of dangerous men, broke up more gangs and sent more fellows away to the pen than any other officer on the frontier. That he took more chances than any other. That he'd been a buffalo hunter and Indian fighter, a government scout and maybe a soldier. That for three tough years he had marshaled Dodge City and never even bothered to reach for his gun till the other guy had hostilities started.

He was not, I thought, the kind of gent for a fellow in my boots to take any tales to. And the more I considered it, the less I liked it.

The talk next morning round the breakfast campfires concerned Sundance—the Sundance Kid. One of the Cantress gang—

Windy Lipari—had just got in with the news from Perry. Sundance was hot on everyone's tongue again. He had pulled two jobs in the space of a night. He had stopped the quartermaster with the Fort Lick payroll and had ransacked Deerfield on the Arkansas River.

The blood money posted on Sundance's scalp had been jumped, dead or alive, to eight thousand dollars.

'Quite a wad of money,' Lipari said; and Concho Corva rolled his eyes.

'There'll be a lot of guys after it,' Charlie allowed.

Andrade looked down his nose and sneered. 'The law'll never put no noose on Sundance, seh,' Hanley declared. 'He's slickeh than slobbers. Not even his own gang knows who he is.'

'Mebbe not,' Charlie said, 'but the price'll get him. Ain't *no* man kin beat a reward like that. You jest watch and see.'

Tulare, across the fire from us, smiled; and I thought again what an odd kind of critter he was to be found in a camp with such godless companions. With his tall, ungainly figure and glasses he looked more like a ranch boss than he did a shoot-or-be-shot member of the owlhooter breed.

Not that you could tell by the look of a guy what he was like inside him. But when a fellow says 'outlaw' you think right away of some glowering, beetle browed cross between a catamount and a she gorilla. You don't think of guys like Charlie and Tulare.

Some of the outlaws had saddled and gone by the time I finished my eating. They had gone with the whiskered Hanley, south, and since their leaving it had seemed to me that an odd kind of quiet had settled over the camp. My companions' looks had turned covert and skittish and every time my glance licked round they appeared to be wholly taken up with the fire, watching its flames with a brooding intensity.

All but Tulare.

Tulare was looking at me. A faint little half smile twisted his lips, when one of the lesser-fry owlhooters came quartering over from the path that led to Cantress' cabin.

'Heard the latest?' he called. His E-string voice fairly shook with excitement and it was plain from his look that his news meant something. 'Some skunk left a law wagon hid in the brush just outside of Perry! Guess y' know what that means, don'tcha? It means Bill Tilghman has called in some help—some deppity we don't know around here!'

Bronc Andrade swore.

'It means, by Gawd,' he said, soft and wicked, 'the star packin' skunk has prob'ly come in disguise an' is ridin' with one of the gangs right now!'

*   *   *

Opening the Indian Nations to settlement was one of the prime contributing factors to the wholesale production of the outlaw gangs which have made Oklahoma notorious. The rank and file of every one of those gangs was made up of men who had earlier been cowboys. They had seen the end of the open range in the farms and fences that were dotting the country. Paved roads and railroads were swiftly replacing the freighter trails and horse paths. Towns were springing up everyplace and the calf roping, horse wrangling cow puncher was finding himself out of a job. Many of these men had gone to Texas, some had gone west to the newer territories—a few had gone north. Some took up land and became sod busters, a few became merchants or star packers. But the bulk of these men—the wilder breed, took to the saddle and six-shooter. They banded themselves together in gangs and hoisted the black flag of piracy. They made a hard, tough crew. Defiant, capable, deadly. It was this kind of breed I was camped with.

Excepting possibly Charlie—and Hanley—who had gone flogging off with the younger bucks—the men lolling round about me were the saltiest hands in Cantress' outfit, quick to anger and quicker to violence.

Like wolves they were, hunched, hunkered

and scowling, licking their tongues across their lips, watching each other slanch-eyed, their finer impulses crushed and trampled under the roughshod impact of the likelihood just exposed by Bronc Andrade.

For most nigh a minute nobody spoke.

Tulare's mouth still held its wry humor.

Corva rolled his eyes with a shrug.

Lipari's hollow tones dropped curses and the frosty air showed the smoke of them sharply.

Charlie, slapping the spit from his harp, said, 'Somebody ort t' kill him. Back in Kaintuck we learned them lawbadges t' mind their own business. Gawd, how I hate the breed! Allus sneakin' an' snoopin' round—put me in mind of a bunch o' damn coyotes!'

Tulare nodded his head, darkly thoughtful. 'For all we know,' he said, 'that packer may be in *this* camp *now*.' And he roved his glass eyed stare around as though he reckoned we might all be candidates. 'Might be callin' himself Concho Corva, mebbe. Or One-Shot Ike or Charlie Kaintuck—'

'Or jes' plain Tulare,' smiled Corva happily.

Tulare ignored him.

I said: 'It don't seem likely he'd pick this outfit. 'F I was a lawman I'd a heap rather get in with Doolin's gang—or with that hellbendin' upstart, Sundance. Anyway, you an' Corva have been around these parts too long to lose any law wagon recent. An' the kid here,

Charlie, ain't hardly had enough experience—'

'*You* ain't got no green round your gills,' butted in Lipari. 'An' you're new to this outfit. What's *yore* alibi?'

And Tulare took off his glasses and looked at me.

I could feel the hair on my neck getting up. But I'd known all along it might come to this. 'Alibi?' I said. 'I ain't offerin' any. I got all the alibi I need right here.' I tapped the butt of my pistol and grinned.

Tulare grinned, too, and shrugged and tramped off.

Corva said, 'Pucha gon undair blanket tonight. That hombre, she's no like you, meester.'

'I'm gonna lose a lot of sleep over that.' I looked at Charlie. 'What've they got on tap for today? This lollin' round's goin' to make me lazy. 'F we don't git some action pretty soon my trigger finger's like to rust off.'

'She's no rost,' the Mexican said with a chuckle. 'Manana, we get the action plenty.'

'Yeah?'

'*Seguro*—sure.' Corva gave me a wink. 'Pretty queeck the Senor Cantress, she's get feex for rob train—no? All the time talk about train with Hanley. Mebbe Doolin, she's rob train, too.'

'If it's action you're cravin',' Charlie mentioned, 'whyn't you start huntin' round f' that knife Cantress lost? He's offerin' a

85

hundred bucks t' the finder, an' no questions ast, neither. Must be settin' a heap of store by it, seems like.'

'What's he got in the handle—map to hidden plunder?'

I saw Lipari's gaunt face come up oddly.

But Corva grinned. 'No, compadre. Thees handle, she ees solid silver. No got nothing in eet. Got shape like the lizard—w'at you call "curio." She's tell me all about heem, one time. Eees hairloom.'

I yawned and allowed I'd go and catch me some shuteye. 'Somethin' about this country,' I said, 'sure makes me sleepy. 'F you turn up that drifting tin-badge anyplace, be sure an' call me. I'd hate mighty bad t' think I'd missed a shot at him.'

Corva was eyeing me, sly and bright like. His mouth was open, kind of, like a bird that's trying to cool his insides off. Kind of smiling, I thought, with the edge of his teeth.

He was smiling, all right.

He give me a wink just before he moved off.

I took my bedroll and went back in the brush. But not to do no damn sleeping. I'd as soon have slept on a railroad track as to shut my eyes again in Sundance Canyon.

*　　　*　　　*

The stars were blinking like departed souls when I sneaked up that night to the shack used by Hanley. He wasn't there—I'd made sure of that. He hadn't been back all day. It seemed a heap likely, considering Corva's talk, that him and the younger bucks were off to a train robbing. But I couldn't help that.

I couldn't help that, but I could take this chance and have a look through his cabin. If any of this crowd had stolen Cantress' silver-handled knife, I'd of bet my shirt the guy's name was Hanley.

The moon wouldn't rise for another hour yet.

Getting that knife back for him looked to me like a mighty good way to put myself solid with the boss of this outfit. It was the best chance, anyway, that I could figure; and it looked like to me, unless I *did* get in with him, *and quick*, somebody's blue whistler would be stopping my clock!

I hadn't forgot that look of Tulare's.

Nor the sly, winking smirk of that Mexican, Corva.

There was other reasons I'd used to persuade me that what I was doing was the shrewdest bet possible.

Unless I was high in Cantress' favor I'd hardly learn anything in time for the knowledge to be of any use to me. I had to have his confidence to bust his gang up—or so, at least, I told myself. And made it sound right plausible, too.

And then, of course, there was the knife

itself.

To tell you the truth, it was the knife decided me. I wanted a look at that lizard handle.

So here I was, sneaking up on the shack Hanley did his sleeping in.

I was all-fired glad I had put in some time making friends of the camp curs. There were two of them now sneaking right along with me. It was God's own mercy they hadn't loosed no yelps.

Like Cantress', Hanley's shack was removed some couple hundred yards from the main part of camp. It set about forty feet to the east of Cantress', which was lighted just now, though the window was blanketed.

I could guess what would happen if Hanley caught me—what would happen, I mean, if *he* had any say in it.

The place wasn't locked. I hadn't thought it would be. But that didn't prove that the knife wasn't in there.

Hanley's shack was the best durn place he could keep it.

I stepped inside and shut the door after me.

The inside was black as a black cat's overcoat.

I hoped the dogs wouldn't whine to get in.

It was then. Right then. It came over me sudden. That I wasn't alone in this curdled murk.

Over yonder there someplace, unseen in the

blackness, there was someone else standing, stealthy quiet and watchful.

I could feel the slow pulse of his throttled-down breathing.

CHAPTER ELEVEN

Cold sweat came out on the back of my neck.

I didn't dare swallow.

My legs felt like they were made of jelly.

There was no sound. Just the slow jerky rasp of that other guy's breathing.

Or, maybe, it was mine.

If the door had been open I expect I'd have bolted. But it wasn't. I had closed it. And now I didn't dare reach for it. I couldn't see the guy, but I'd bet my last cent he had a gun pointed at me. Or a knife.

Let me move so much as the fifth part of an eyelash.

The pulsing quiet became insupportable.

With a sudden rush the fellow was into me—into me and past me, wrenching the door open. His rush had taken me unawares. His hurtling shoulder had smashed the breath from me, spun me gasping against the wall. But I threw myself after him—clutched at him desperately. Felt his perked clothing skid loose of my fingers.

I saw the black shape of him limned against

starlight.

I flung open the door. I tried to get my jammed gun out, and heard the two curs tearing round with wild yelpings. One, dashing inside, struck my leg. I went lurching.

That off-balance stagger was all that saved me.

Through a night come suddenly alive with voices I heard the *swish* of something bite past me. A pistol barrel, aimed for my head, came down with a crash on the slant of my shoulder. I went down like a wall that a mule has kicked over.

But I knew what was coming. I didn't wait for it. I lit flat and kept rolling till I was into the brush with the dull thump of bullets spatting dust all around me.

'There he goes! Off to the left there!'

I heard a horse coming lickety-split; and Corva's voice, excited, yell: *'Quien es? Quien es?*—Who een hell ees it?'

'I dunno,' snarled Charlie, 'but we better git 'im!' And the horse tore past, and somebody said, 'What the hell was he doin' in Hanley's cabin?' And before any of them could answer that, Cantress' cool tones was rasping out orders.

'Bend left—over there. Bend more to the left. He's in those trees—he's makin' for the horses.'

I heard the gang go larruping east of me. It looked like a damn good time to get out of there.

I commenced working west through the brush, real careful, keeping well down. I thought if I could get a bit north, up beyond Cantress' cabin, I could swing a big circle and come back from the south. Like I'd just woke up and wanted in on the fun.

I wished I knew who that other guy was. He was slicker than bear grease. I'll say that much for him. Diving out frantic, then laying in wait for me. It was God's own mercy I wasn't brained. I got pretty near to my circle starting when a couple ideas begun to take me in hand.

I couldn't tell if Cantress had steered the gang off my track deliberately or if he really figured I was over in them trees. But I was willing to bet that he'd done it on purpose.

If he had, he had probably guessed who I was—guessed I mean, it was me. Guessed what I was up to. The more I thought on it the likelier it seemed. I poked up my head to see how the land lay. And there, square before me, was the face of Bronc Andrade. I knew it was him by the glow of his cigarette.

He saw me right off. And was bringing his gun up, with his lantern-jawed mouth opening wide for a bellow, when I caught him a head jolting pop with my right. It was a beautiful blow and it paid for a lot of things. By the sparks from his quirly I saw him rock backwards, saw the sag of his face muscles—his black, bulging eyes. I hit him again; and saw the brush swallow him.

He'd be out anyways for at least twenty minutes. I'd smacked guys before. He'd keep just as good as a hog on ice; and, meantime, Hanley's cabin was empty, and the gang was off snorting around in them trees, a good hundred yards or more off and away from it.

'What the hell!' I said. I wouldn't be getting no *better* chance.

You can make yourself believe almost anything. If it happens you're wanting to bad enough. And I still was wanting a look at that knife.

So bad I could taste it.

*   *   *

There was nothing between me and Hanley's cabin but a stretch of weeds. Waist high. Just right to conceal me. Till the moon came up.

I figured I had another quarter hour.

Plenty of time to go through that cabin.

I crouched down. I crawled through the weeds like a goddam monkey. Off east, beyond the tangle of cottonwoods, I could hear the calls and quips of the hunters. By the sound they were about fed up with their hunting. They was also considerably farther away.

I come out of the weeds by the back of the cabin. And I looked around for a good couple minutes before I lifted myself into sight. I guessed my figuring was pretty good, this time.

The cabin was quiet. It was black inside, just like I'd remembered. The door was still open. I didn't hear any breathing.

I made sure my belt gun was loose in its holster, and went on in. It was black, all right. I couldn't even see my hand in front of me. I began feeling around.

It was creepy business. What I needed was a light, but I couldn't well strike one with that door standing open. Maybe, if I pushed it to—But, no, that wasn't going to help none. The light of a match would show through the windows. It would bring that gang tearing back in a hurry.

I guessed I would have to wait for the moon.

Though I'd persuaded myself nobody'd expect me to come back again, I *had* come back.

And somebody else might.

The guy I'd walked in on might figure like I had. He'd figured like I had before, evidently. He'd sure enough figured Hanley had Cantress' knife! Else why had he been here?

Thinking like that wasn't soothing my nerves none.

The best place to wait was back of the door, so if someone came in I would have the drop on them.

I got back of it. And waited.

It seemed like the moon wouldn't ever come up.

I wasn't going to wait much longer, I told

myself. My scheme didn't look even near so good now. I heard a scampering yonder and tiny, bright eyes made a glint through the murk. Pack rat, probably.

I felt like a fool. I said I was a fool, likely. A brash, headlong fool or I'd not have come back here.

I stepped away from the wall, half deciding to go, when a shaft of moonlight struck through the back window.

That knife got the best of me. I decided to hunt for it.

I was bending over Hanley's warsack when something lifted the hairs on my neck. I don't know yet what it was that warned me, but my acts were instinctive. I whirled both hands clawing for a gun.

I never touched them.

A man stood lounged in the open doorway. He was watching me smugly across a pistol.

*   *   *

We stared at each other for a half dozen heartbeats.

'Some time,' I said toughly, 'you'll git shot tryin' that stunt.'

It was the glass-eyed Tulare.

He grinned at me smugly.

I said, 'Put up that gun an' give me a hand here. I'm tryin' to make out what that fella was up to. Don't look like he got nothin'.'

94

Tulare eyed me a moment longer, then pulled up his shoulders out of their slouch and gave his gun a few twirls by the trigger guard.

He moved to one side and Corva came in.

Corva looked at me, knowing like.

'Cool customer, ain't he?' Tulare remarked.

I said, 'That ain't the tone to be took with me, bucko. Give me a hand or get the hell outa here.'

In the brightening light coming through the back window I could see pretty clear how they figured they had me.

I thought so myself. But there's times when a bluff looks better than four aces.

'C'mon,' I said. 'Either roll your cotton or get busy an' help me!'

Corva flashed me a grin. 'Like the chunk of ice. Like the—w'at you call?—cucumbair!'

Tulare sneered. 'To a bullet a cucumber's no better than a pickle. I say—'

'*Nada*,' Corva told him. 'That ees not the way for get blood from turnip. I'm savvy thees One-Shot plenty. You,' he said to me, 'are een thees gang for same theeng we are; for w'at she ees wort' to you—no? *Sta 'ueno!* We make heem wort' *muchas*. Thees Cantress, she ees not'eeng to you. *Bueno!* Not'eeng to thees man—not'eeng to me.'

He rolled back his lips with a quick flash of teeth.

'*Pues, muerto—Ai!* Dead, them Cantress she ees wort' *muchas dinero*—Mebbeso five t'ousan' dollar!'

He looked at me slanchways, head cocked to one side. 'You keel—no?'

I said, 'Lemme get this straight. You're wantin' Cantress put outa the way. You're suggestin' I do it. That the idea?'

Corva's tongue made a licking swipe at his lips. His moistened mouth parted to disclose his white teeth again. '*Segur' Miguel! Si!*'

'An' you'll pay me five thousand for doin' it, eh?'

'*Si*—w'en them Cantress she ees *muerto*.'

'Any pa'tic'lar way I should do it?'

'The way, we leave to you, senor.'

'An' suppose I don't care to have no part in it?'

'We ain't goin' to suppose that,' Tulare said.

I looked at Corva. Corva grinned brightly.

'What about the gang,' I said—'the rest of the outfit? Mebbe they won't be likin' this jamboree.'

'We take care of that, my frien'.'

'Got it all figured out, eh? Well,' I said, 'I'm afraid I ain't interested.'

The muzzle of Tulare's pistol tilted. A hard, cold glint suddenly shone from his eyes. Corva leaned forward, put his face close to mine. His fingers put a clamp like claws on my arm. 'You weel be interes', my frien', or you weel be ver-ry dead. *Muerto*—you savvy?'

'*Los salvajes*, eh? An' what's to prevent me from spreadin' this story?'

96

'In the first place,' Tulare chucked in, 'there wouldn't be nobody believe you. You'd be wastin' your breath.'

'An'' said Corva, tightening his grip, but keeping out of the way of Tulare's pistol, 'you won', because eef you do . . .' he grinned and drew a slow finger across his throat.

Well, after all, what the hell! I thought. Cantress was one of the owlhoot crew I was supposed, by my orders, to help Bill Tilghman clean out of this country. If I killed him I'd not be doing any more than my duty. He would hang sure as hell if Judge Parker got hold of him.

Just the same . . .

'You weel do like we tell you,' declared Corva convincingly, 'because we 'ave caught you weeth the—w'at you call?—*goods*. Because een town you 'ave keel Benson by Teelghman's offeece—'

'An' if you don't kill Cantress,' pronounced Tulare slyly, 'that O'Daye skirt's goin' to have to marry him to save her ol' man's bacon—savvy?'

That was the straw. It let the wind clean out of me. I could only stand there and gape. With my mouth open.

Corva grinned. '*Es verdad*—trut'. Two nights from now. She weel marry heem—*sangre de cristo*—yes! Or else—'

'He'll send ol' O'Daye up fer life,' Tulare said.

97

Corva said with a leer, 'You keel them Cantress?'

I must have looked like a boxhead, proper. I couldn't seem to get hold of myself. But what could I say?

I finally nodded.

''*Sta bueno*,' said Corva, and patted my shoulder. 'You use the *cabesa*. W'en them Cantress she's dead, mebbe *you* be *capitan*. Be *rico*; 'ave the *muchas dinero* to shake een the pockets—'ave senorita. *Muy bueno!*'

'And,' Tulare grinned, 'to bind the bargain we'll give you the knife—I guess that oughta show who your friends are.'

And there, on the palm of his extended left hand, hilt towards me and gleaming in the window-thrown moonglow, was the missing 'heirloom'—Cantress' silver lizard knife.

CHAPTER TWELVE

The manhunters had got all done with their hunting when I finally come out of the Texan's cabin.

I'd cached the knife out of sight in my boot. I could feel it again my shins like a branding iron.

It occurred to me, now I'd got the thing, I better leave it alone. Packing it round was like packing dynamite. Only worse. With a little

98

plain care you was safe with dynamite.

I had sure got me into a fine mess now!

What was that line Hanley'd handed Cantress? 'Find the knife and we'll have the rascal!'

I'd never thought to find Hanley a prophet.

Trouble was, I hadn't *thought.*

But I was thinking now. I was thinking *plenty.* If I didn't get out of this camp damn quick, I was like to be planted here. Surer than sin.

'Well,' purred Tulare, 'what's eatin' you now?'

I said, 'When you wantin' I should do this for you?'

'It ain't fer *me* you're doin' it, bucko!'

I heard Corva chuckle. 'We weel let you know.'

Tulare's voice was a low, hard rasp. 'You keep your hands off him till we give you the word.'

It was a trap all right. I felt like a guy on the thirteenth step of the Fort Smith scaffold.

If there was any one thing I could still depend on, it was the extreme probability I'd leave my bones here.

I wondered what Ed Cantress would say if I spilled my guts to him. About the hunch I'd got of Hanley having his knife; about my searching Hanley's cabin, and the upshot of it.

Like he'd read my thoughts Tulare said: 'Until you get the word you keep plumb away

99

from him—savvy?'

'What do you mean by that?'

'I guess you know. If you want to get planted, just try double-crossing us.'

We rejoined the others round the rekindled campfire.

I squatted down with my back to a cottonwood. Charlie, right doleful, was blowing *Sweet Fern* again. I stared at the flames but I didn't see them. I didn't even listen to the comments and guesses that was being passed round about the prowler's identity. I had identity problems of my own.

I started off. I had just recollected that Andrade pelican. And what he was like to do when we met again. Likewise what he would say if it happened some other guy met up with him first.

I didn't need to squint through Tulare's glasses to know my days were damn well numbered if I didn't get out of this camp *muy pronto*. But how—how to get out? That was the problem. Then, just as I turned, a lucky thought struck me.

I might cut it yet.

I wheeled to look back at the group in the fireglow. 'Where's Andrade?' I said, and the bunch went still. 'You reckon, by grab, he coulda been the one . . .?'

Lipari said: 'Christ!'

'Hi gee! It *coulda* been him! I seen him snoopin' round over there—,' another allowed.

'Where the hell's he at now?'

They swapped quick looks, sharp with suspicion.

Corva give me a wink.

Charlie heaved himself up and took a squint at his hardware. 'C'mon,' he said, 'let's hunt the damn sidewinder!'

I began to feel better when I see they was for it. Let them once get scattered, prowling round through the dark, and I'd soon have a horse and be dusting the high spots.

I knew who was who in this Cantress gang now and the quicker I sheared loose of them the sooner we could grab them.

I expect I'm about as brave as the average, but a quitting time comes to every man's hand. The best of luck will only stretch so far. Time to get out was right now—tonight. Tomorrow might prove to be a little too late.

As for Betsy O'Daye and her prospective nuptials . . . I could help her in town a lot better than here.

Corva'd told me they were figuring to rob a train. I remembered the dope I had to get to Bill Tilghman. I recollected what Corva had said about Benson.

Now was the time to go, all right.

'Mebbe,' I said, 'I better check on them horses—'

The sound of shod hoofs was coming out of the south. Two riders, I figured, coming fast.

I heard them hit hardpan and slosh through

the creek bed, heard the curs unlimber a lusty yelping.

Tulare backed swiftly out of the firelight. 'Just a sec, fellas. Let's see who this is—'

I had seen already.

That whiskered buffalo—that Texan, Hanley.

And Betsy was with him.

It was then that Bronc Andrade come out of the shadows.

CHAPTER THIRTEEN

What, at first, I had took for a blaze of excitement in Hanley's eyes looked different now that I saw him closer. It was not excitement; it was triumph—a jubilant impudence fanned brighter and brighter by something malicious that was locked in his mind.

I watched his sly glance shuttle over to Andrade; come swift-streaking back with its reckless mirth heightened. It made my guts turn over—*sudden.*

This was going to be it. In my bones I knew it.

I was trapped all right. I was trapped right proper. I had put off my leaving a little too long.

Somebody yowled: 'Where the hell you

102

been, Bronc?'

Andrade ignored him. He was looking at me. I could tell by his eyes he knew who had smacked him.

There was a brash grin twisting his firelit features. A hank of black hair dangled over his forehead. His spraddled right hand was just over his gun stock.

It was Hanley, though, that opened his mouth first.

'Mister *Stroud*,' he said. 'I'm sho' glad t' see you—woulda laid good money I'd be findin' you flown.'

I guessed he'd been talking with Pierce and Newcomb. Or had someway wangled the truth out of Betsy . . .

Her eyes were like holes in her white, pulled tight features. Reaching across to me, pleading and miserable—like she was eating her heart out for what she had done for me.

'Flown—' I said; but Charlie broke in with his face all scowling.

'"Stroud" did you say? You callin' that at One-Shot?'

'I ain't undehtakin' t' desc'ibe his ancestors—'

'Yo' crazy as hell!' Charlie roared. He glared, baleful, one hand half dropped to the butt of his pistol.

I said: 'Keep out of this, Charlie. I can gut my own hawgs.'

He never even looked at me. His slanchways

glance was combing Hanley.

'You tryin' t' have us think ol' One-Shot's the star-packin' deppity of that buzzard, Heck Thomas?'

'You called the tu'n, button.'

I was just on the edge of unshucking my hardware when Betsy's voice, bitter sharp and impatient, cut angrily into the Texan's talking.

'Him?' she cried, her eyes raking me scornful. The sweep of her hand was indignant—intolerant. 'That's not the fellow! He don't even *look* like him!'

She flung around on Hanley, scathing, contemptuous.

'Did I heah you correctly, girl?' You could see the black fury creeping up through his whiskers. 'D'you stan' theah an' tell me—'

'I've a notion,' she said, 'to go and tell Ed of this! I guess you know what *he'd* say about it—dragging me out here—'

'Shut yo' blat,' Hanley snarled, 'an' anseh my question! Is—'

'I've already answered it. He's not here, I told you.' Her bright glance swept the circle of faces. 'There's nobody here that even faintly resembles him!'

I could have hugged her!

The look of that Texan was something for wolves to see. His teeth clamped shut. His whiskered face purpled and swelled and bloated. Looked like he'd pop if he got any madder.

'Yo' mean t' say—'

'Are you trying to call me a *liar*, Hanley?'

I tell you that girl was magnificent. Where she got such gall was away beyond me; but if I hadn't known better I'd believed her myself! With her bright gold hair flying loose and wild, chin up, head lifted, she was like a young filly, contemptuous of man traps.

You could see mighty plain the gang believed her. Charlie's drawl lazed across the grumbles. 'Better be beggin' her pahdon, Hanley—an' you kin beg One-Shot's, whiles you're at it, too.'

'That's all right,' I said, feeling generous.

It was then Bronc Andrade shoved his oar in.

I'd forgot all about him, admiring Betsy.

He'd not forgot me.

He was crouched just behind me, not three foot off, with a gun in his fist and his squinched eyes gleaming.

'It don't make no difference,' he said, 'what his name is—he's the cockeyed varmint that stole Ed's knife!'

*   *   *

One flat moment of silence followed.

A cold, thin silence that got tight and wicked. A vacuum suddenly, explosively broken.

My fist took Andrade square in the mouth.

105

He reeled, stumbling backward, against the locked circle. He lost his gun as the men threw him back at me. I heard Betsy's gasp—heard the whistle of breath through the gap where Bronc's teeth had been.

He got his boots under him and come for me, snarling. I stopped Andrade's leap with a smash to the temple. Gave him another while he hung there, groggy.

Stunned and half-blinded he blundered into me. I give him a hook that was brought up from my bootstraps. He went backwards and crumpled like a horse fell on him.

'Anyone else—' I was starting to say, when I saw the blur of the Texan's gun hand.

Firelight danced off the wink of metal. Flame was a lance in a halo of gun smoke.

I knew I was falling but I could not stop it.

CHAPTER FOURTEEN

'Plumb center!' yelled Lipari. 'I guess you split that pumpkin roller!'

'Well—' Tulare growled. 'What are you waitin' on? Ain't scared you missed, are you?'

'I don't miss,' Hanley said; and whatever else might have been on his tongue was lost in the sudden outbreak of shouting. The ground gave back a thud of boots. Muttered oaths and questions mingled. The voice of Cantress crossed them grimly.

'What's goin' on here?'

'I been riddin' this camp of a goddam spy, seh!'

'Since when did I give you care of this camp?'

Cantress' tones was soft and wicked. But Hanley told him, brash with bluster: 'You can't go galley-hootin' round afteh women an'—'

'*Can't!* Are you presuming to tell Ed Cantress—'

'Ain't perzoomin' nothin'—'

'—how to run this outfit? You,' Cantress said, 'that's lost four hauls to Sundance hand-running?'

There was growls and grumbling; and Hanley snarled, 'I seen a snake an' I shot 'is damn head off! An' whiles I'm at it—'

'You'll put that gun up. Put it up right now. Any orders given out in this camp, *I'll* given 'em. By grab, if that's One-Shot—'

'That's a damn, sneakin' tin-packin' spy!'

'That's—' began Cantress, when through his talk Hanley's choked voice blared:

'By Gawd, I'll have my say onct! Thet galoot's Ike Stroud—a Fort Smith! Heck Thomas' deputy! I got the—'

'You've got more gall than Sundance Kid,' Betsy cried, 'to stand there brazen and lie to Ed like that!'

Conflicting growls came out of the men. Someone said: 'Hanley fetched her here t' prove it up on him—'

'*An*',' drawled Charlie, 'we all heard her tell 'im it wasn't One-Shot—'

'Ye heared what Andrade said, didn't ye?'

'Enough!' Cantress snapped. 'Hush your wrangling and put up that gun, Hanley. I'll have no more fighting around this camp. Go turn Ike over. We'll see what we can do for him—'

'Come he ain't got enough, I'll *do* for him,' Hanley said. 'I'll se'ch 'im, too,' whiles I'm at it. Andrade claimed—'

Charlie said, 'Andrade's been jealous of him ever sinct that shootin' match.'

There was a second of silence. Then Cantress said, 'Turn him over.'

I could feel Hanley's breath wheeze across my cheek. His hand grabbed a hold on my shoulder. He braced himself with a grunt and heaved. As my shoulderblades came against the ground I looked up into his whiskers and laughed.

His eyes bugged out like they was knots on a stick. What skin I could see went gray as putty.

I had the snout of my belly gun looking right at him.

Cantress said, 'By grab!' through a chorus of gasps.

Charlie come over.

'You bad hurt, pard?'

'You funnin' me, Charlie? That whiskered ape,' I said with a sneer, 'couldn't hurt a June frost! Got me beat what Ed keeps him round for. A five-year-old kid—'

'Damn yo' eyes!' Hanley choked. 'I've a good mind—'

'Time you was usin' it then,' I said. I grabbed his hand and pulled myself up.

He snatched loose his paw with a burst of profanity. Sent it streaking, snarling, for the butt of his six-shooter.

'Well, well!' I said, and put away my pistol. 'Go right ahead! Git your tail up, polecat.'

It looked like he would. But he didn't, some way. He stood froze a minute, then fished out the makings and built him up a brown paper smoke.

'The's a Yank phrase, seh, thet fits yo' case.'

The tone of his voice gave his words dark meaning. But I could see he wasn't going to leave it there. A black rage was churning him, pounding him, spurring him.

''Bout foolin' folks,' he said, thick and nasty. 'The's folks you kin fool right smaht, this Yank said—'

'You don't have to quote Abe Lincoln at me. If it's the matter of that knife you're fixin' to get at, trot it out in the open an' lay your talk straight—'

'I'll lay it straight, you white livehed tinbadge! These boys all heard Bronc put the name to you. *He* told you straight! Said you had thet knife an'—'

'What knife?'

109

That was Cantress' voice, sharp, suspicious.

'An' it ain't thet knife *only*,' growled the Texan, wicked. 'The's a heap o' things round heah mahked with yo' label—'

'What knife?' Cantress' look was impatient.

'Your knife,' I said. 'With the lizard handle. Andrade told 'em I had it.'

'Have you?'

'You wanta search me?' I said.

He looked at me slanchways. Then he said real soft: 'Not if you say you ain't got it. I'll take your word—'

'The word of a damn tinbadge! Why, thet cotton mouth sidewindeh killed Benson yestiday! Never give 'im no chanct nor nothin'!' Hanley gritted. 'Shoved a gun in 'is belly an' let 'im have it!'

'Who says so?'

'*I* say so!'

'How about it, Ike?'

'Sure I killed him,' I said. 'You'd have killed him yourself if you'd been in my boots. I come on him smackdab in front of Tilghman's office.'

'You been wonderin',' I said, 'who the spy was round here. If you don't know now, I guess you never will.'

*   *   *

Hard to tell what needs and notions inside a man's head go to shape his actions. When you

110

see life's end but a few jumps away there ain't much counts beside the wish to keep living. Instinct governs a man such times, I reckon.

I could see one thing almighty plain: I had got to get loose of that camp—get *quick.* To linger longer would be same as suicide.

I got to thinking again about that knife in my boot—Cantress' knife that Tulare had give me to show his good faith.

I wondered what it was Cantress had in that handle. Map of hidden plunder? Didn't hardly seem like a man could get much more than that in it. That lizard grip wasn't barely long enough to give a good hold on it, and not even its belly was sufficiently thick to hold much more than three bills rolled up. Solid silver, Cantress had said. So had Corva—but that was all my eye. There was something in it. Or there must have been sometime, else Cantress wouldn't be wanting it back so.

It looked screwy—screwy as hell, Tulare passing that knife to me. Unless he had already got at its secret.

I thought a bit then. Maybe that was it— maybe he couldn't come at it; and they were passing it to me to see if *I* could do it.

I had tried once already without no luck. It *seemed* to be solid.

It come to me then I had ought to give it to Cantress and put myself solid with him. But I didn't figure to give up that knife till I seen what was in it.

The smart thing for me was to roll my hocks out of here. I made up my mind I was going to—pronto.

But just as I come easing onto my feet, thinking the camp settled all it was like to be, there come a scrunching sound. Like a boot on loose gravel.

I stared through the black with the sweat pouring out of me. Was it Corva? Tulare?

A tight, choked-up whisper come out of the darkness.

'Ike! Is that you?'

I had plumb forgot Bet O'Daye was still out there.

CHAPTER FIFTEEN

'What you doin' here?' I said. A lot harsher, probably than I had any right to. But I'd kept my voice down.

So did she. 'I ain't had much chance to get away, have I? Besides, I had to see you first. I—I had to find out if you *are* an officer.'

'So you could go back an' tell Cantress— that it?'

It was a heap too dark for me to see her face. I could only just barely make out the shape of her; but I heard the gasp of the breath she drew into her.

I felt my ears get hot. I hadn't no call to slap

that kind of talk at her even if she *was* figuring to marry Ed Cantress. She wasn't getting hitched up with him because she wanted to.

It give me a twist to think what a boor I'd been. After all, if it hadn't been for her . . .

I said: 'Reckon I'm owin' you a mite of thanks. For what you said at the fire tonight.'

It was funny—me saying them words, I mean. They wasn't at all what I'd set out to say. She had helped me plenty and I'd meant to tell her so. Seemed like I couldn't noways make talk to her without I made a damn fool of myself.

'Well, you know . . . I heard what those men said to you—'

'Then you heard what I told them, too, didn't you? Told 'em, by God, I was all through with that stuff—'

'But you didn't figure to mean it—not really.'

I stared at her sharply. But I couldn't see nothing but the vague, dark shape of her. 'How do you know what I meant?' I said.

'Well-l . . . I been hoping you didn't.'

In the gloom her voice sounded sad, sort of tired like. Kind of low and faint, like she hadn't got hardly no more breath than it took to get the words up out of her.

It did give me a twist, but I kept my mouth shut. If she wanted to talk, that was all right with me. But I wasn't spilling *my* guts around.

'. . . been hoping you didn't,' she said,

113

'because—because I thought, perhaps, between the two of us, we might be able to wreck this gang.'

'You thought *what*!' I said. I wished the hell I could see her face. But the night was too black, too heavy with shadows.

But I knew she'd come closer. You could smell the clean smell of her—the soft, woman smell. I felt the touch of her hand on my arm, and a strange, queasy feeling hit the pit of my belly. A tremble got hold of me. I could feel my knees shaking.

Then she said, kind of hushed, kind of odd and wishful, 'Do—do you think that's too crazy—too wild and unlikely? We could do it—I feel sure we could do it, between us.' She tightened her grip on my arm, said more eager: 'I've got it all thought out. You could tell Ed Cantress—or I could tell him, either one—the stage company's holding a big haul of bullion at its office in town. We could say that, to keep down suspicion, they've only put one guard to watching it—an old man with a shotgun. You and Uncle Bill could have a posse ready; thrown all around in those shacks by the stage office, and when the gang comes in you'd have them trapped. It's—why it's almost fool proof!'

It did have a sound, the way she told it.

I don't know what the matter was with me, but all I could think of was her and Ed Cantress—Cantress, with his arms clamped round her, like I'd seen him in that moonlit clearing. But her plan was cute—it was too damned cute. It wasn't fitting in a woman to think up such things . . .

And then it came to me. Maybe she hadn't thought it up; maybe somebody else had thought it up for her. Cantress, maybe. He'd been wanting to get rid of Hanley's faction— leastways, I would of been if I'd been in his boots. Be a damn good way for him to do it, too. He could send Hanley in—him and all his cronies; and Tilghman would damn well see they stayed there. Stayed there or stepped off the Fort Smith gallows.

But it wouldn't do to let her see I was onto it.

I said: 'What's all this got to do with you?'

'Do you think I *want* to marry Ed Cantress?'

Her tone was sharp, her words quick and flat; but I said, 'I don't see you have any call to marry him.'

Through the gloom I could sense the shake of her head. 'You don't understand! He's got some kind of hold on my uncle—something my uncle has done, or been framed for—'

'If your uncle ain't done nothin' he'll get out of it all right.'

'You don't know Ed Cantress! The things he thinks up—Oh, he's evil—evil! Plain nasty and vile!' she said, shuddering. 'Some times I think he's . . . he isn't *human*.'

I saw her shoulders drop, heard her sigh. 'I

115

can't make you see him. If you were a girl, you'd know . . . Tomorrow night—or some other night soon, he's going to rob a train—he just told me about it. We'll be married first. There's a preacher in town. Some Baptist revivalist. They're going to bring him out here, or stop by in town on their way to the holdup. We're to celebrate our *marriage* by stopping this train—he says the Daltons pulled the same thing here last year. But it's no crazy lark,' she said bitterly. 'He's doing it to put me in with the rest of them; to tie my hands and keep my mouth shut. We'll be masked, of course, but I'm to wear a short riding skirt. He wants them to know I'm a woman. I'm to go through the coaches and "frisk" the passengers . . .'

She sighed again. Dispirited, hopeless.

It didn't seem right for a girl like her to be at the end of her rope that way.

I could feel the pull of her tugging me, calling me. Some way or other it scared me, sudden like. I'd felt that kind of hunger before. Cow camps is full of it. Always been my brag I could take a woman or leave her be.

But I got to wondering . . .

Come over me sudden that maybe I couldn't. That maybe I hadn't been tried before. That I was just as damn ornery as any guy around me.

'Women,' I said, 'make their bargains—'

'Bargains!'

She come round like I'd struck her.

'Don't you call it bargainin' to tie up with Cantress?'

'Do you think,' she blazed, 'I'd tie up with him if—'

'Well? If what?'

'If there was any way round it!'

She was mad, all right—plain mad as a diamondback.

And it looked like she meant it.

But I had to be sure.

'There's a way,' I said.

I could feel her eyeing me.

'What way?' she whispered.

'I might kill him,' I said.

*   *   *

She was still for so long I got to figuring she hadn't heard me.

But she had. With a kind of lilt to her voice she asked: 'Do you reckon you could do it, Ike?'

It took me back—took me back aplenty. Don't ask me what I'd been expecting. I hadn't allowed for nothing like that. Never in all my gun wrangling days had I reckoned to hear that kind of talk come out of a woman.

'Do you reckon you could do it?' she says.

Like killing guys was crumpling paper!

And her so young and sweet and shy!

When I figured to trust my voice, I said,

'You're sure that's the way you're wantin' it?'

She kind of loosed a shiver then. 'It's not what I want, Ike.' She sighed. 'My uncle don't count. It's what will be good for this country— for this new Oklahoma that's just been born; that's what we've got to keep our minds on. The greatest good for the greatest number.'

Crazy—that's what her talk was. Batty!

I said, 'I could make a stab at it.'

'Would you?'

I didn't know whether I would or not. Her, and the night, seemed to be warping my judgment. We were both making talk, but no one was listening. I felt like a guy with a full load of likker.

A pebble scrunched—she had come in closer. I could tell by her breathing she felt same as I did.

I said, quick and gruff, 'You ever been kissed?'

The night was too much for me.

Before she could move, I had my hands on her.

I kissed her—hard.

Her hair came loose. It run down over my hands like water.

CHAPTER SIXTEEN

The lone trails breed fierce hungers in a man. I lost all count of time, surroundings. I banged my head on the rim of the world.

'Ike!'

It come to me sudden she wasn't liking this. She had got her hands up and was pounding me, scratching me. The heave of her breath sounded choked and wheezy.

*　　*　　*

'You got to get outa here,' I told her finally.

She nodded, meek like.

'I'll take care of Cantress,' I said, 'but first off, I'm going to make sure you git clear of this camp. I aim to go with you, but come I ain't able, you're to hit out for town—an' don't be stoppin' to pick no posies. Take this note. I want you to see that it gets to Bill Tilghman— pers'nal. Take it yourself just as quick as you get there. Then go to your uncle's store and wait for me. Savvy?'

I saw the shake of her head in the darkness. Felt her shiver.

'Maybe,' she said, 'if we get out of here together it won't come to guns between you and Cantress. After he hears we've been married—'

'Don't fool yourself! This crowd won't rest till they've seen me planted—or done their best to. But never mind that,' I said, quick like. 'The thing to be kept in your mind right now is to get that note to Bill Tilghman, pronto. No matter what happens you see that he gets it. Understand?'

'All right. But we'll make it.'

She tucked her hand snug inside my arm and we moved through the felted gloom of the junipers.

We'd come out of the trees by the big corral. You could hear the horses—not twenty foot off—you could see two or three toss their heads, turn towards us.

There they was, just back of the corral's peeled poles.

And parked by the gate was a guy to watch them.

I could see the red glow of his cigarette.

He was looking right at us. But it didn't seem likely he could make us out. Not with all the black trees back of us.

I put my mouth to Betsy's ear. 'There's a guard over there, but I'll take care of him. You slip around back—off beyond them horses.'

'They'll nicker!'

Fright and excitement tightened her grip on me.

I got myself loose of it. 'Never mind that. You do what I say. Be saddled stock tied around here someplace; Cantress' always got

three-four head up. You find them broncs an'
stick right with 'em. 'F you hear any trouble git
on one an' run for it.'

She didn't much cotton to it—didn't like it
at all.

I could feel her shaking.

'Ike—'

'Go on,' I said.

The darkness swallowed her.

I looked for the guard. Couldn't find him—
couldn't see his cigarette, even.

A dry voice said right behind my elbow,
'You wasn't figurin' to be leavin' us, was you?'

CHAPTER SEVENTEEN

I didn't slam round.

I knew a deal better than to try any fast
stuff.

That voice was Tulare's. Tulare's hand
would be holding a pistol.

I turned around casual. 'What the hell
would I leave for?'

'What, indeed!' he said nasty, and laughed.
Injun laughter. 'Come along,' he told me.

I stood where I was. 'Come where? An'
what for?'

'For saddle op, One-Shot.'

That was Corva's voice. On the other side of
me.

I wondered how long them two bucks had been standing there.

'What kind of game you fellas up to?'

'No game. By dam', she's de Cantress' ordairs—Come! We get *los caballos* . . .'

His voice trailed off and he stood cocked, listening.

I knew what he heard. A kind of stifled groan. I'd heard it myself. If I'd had any wits I could of covered what was coming by wagging my jaw or maybe starting a rumpus—anything, almost, so it served to screen it.

But I hadn't. And I didn't. Betsy's move had been too wicked fast, pummeling my ears with the crashing of brush, with the racketing pound of a ridden horse leaving.

Gouts of flame left Tulare's bent shape, the reports of his gun sound beating the night, drowning all else with its wild, thrumming thunder, droning the dark with its death winged lead.

The camp curs came running, adding their range of yelps to the uproar. Everywhere the gloom seemed pocked with the quick jerking shapes of men jumped from their blankets. Shouts and curses crisscrossed the shadows.

'Come! We go now,' muttered Corva, and took down his rope from a hull on the kak pole. He shook out his loop and slipped through the bars, Tulare and me following suit with our own ropes. If there had been other horses standing under saddle, Betsy, in leaving, had wisely stampeded them.

We led our captured stock from the corral, piled the gear on and bridled it. A lot of the owlhooters were still milling round, shouting questions and curses as they prowled through the gloom.

Tulare grunted. 'This way,' he said, 'an' mind your step.'

We came out of the trees at Cantress' cabin. A man and two broncs was waiting in front of it. 'That you, Anson?'

'No. It's me—Lipari. Who's that you got with you?'

'One-Shot an' Corva. Chief ready?'

Cantress came out, slammed the door shut behind him. 'Where's Andrade?'

'Here,' said the Bronc, reining up on my left.

A strained sense of waiting, of something between them, marked the silent shapes of the Chief and Tulare.

'Well?' Cantress snapped it finally; said it short and impatient.

'She give us the slip,' Tulare said gruffly. 'Was her, ridin' off, that unloosed all that racket.'

Cantress swung to his saddle without no comment.

'Where we off to?' I said.

'You'll find out when we get there.'

*　　　*　　　*

123

I had a good idea before we got there.

My hunch was right.

But somewhere there had been a switch in the plans. Probably caused, I thought, by Betsy's flight. We didn't ride into Perry as planned; we walked our broncs clear around the town, keeping well away from its noise and light. We pulled up by the stockyards, a half mile south, leaving Lipari to hold the horses.

It was not far to daylight.

False dawn was already graying the sky when we dropped down into the cindered hollow that, all along here, flanked the right-of-way. Tulare went scrambling up the bank with his neckerchief pulled up over his cheekbones.

I wondered if Betsy had found Bill Tilghman.

I saw Ed Cantress get out his watch and, holding it close to his face, take a look at it. They were going to stop the Texas Express.

There didn't seem to be much I could do about it. Not with Corva and Andrade both watching me. I remembered the edgy shortness that had marked Cantress' manner when I'd asked him where we was off to. Looked like his opinion of me might be changing.

'Ten minutes,' he said, glancing up from his ticker.

There was a steel tower reared beside the

tracks. A green light gleamed from its semaphore. Tulare was a dark blotch over the hand switch.

When the Express hit this point it was the engineer's practice, Corva said, to whistle.

Cantress was taking no chances. He stood by the tower with his watch in hand. He'd the point of a shoulder against the steel uprights—the only one of our crowd not masked.

After awhile he nodded, slow like.

'Three minutes,' he said; and Corva went catfooting up to the tracks and put an ear against one of the rails.

I thought it was queer Hanley hadn't come with us.

We could see Tulare crouched by the signal.

Horse sound came suddenly down from above us. The creak of gear. The jingle of spur chains. The shapes of three riders came over the cutbank. A damn bad taste come up from my gizzard. The riders was Charlie, Trigger Hanley and Betsy.

*   *   *

Hanley eyed Cantress and spat through his whiskers.

'Damn you,' Cantress said. 'Didn't I tell you to leave your broncs by the—'

'My suggestion,' tucked in Charlie smoothly. 'Wasn't no time t' come around by the stockyards. Main thing was t' git here. We figgered t' do it.'

'What've you done with the preacher?'

'Left him tied up in a draw back yonder.'

'You *fools*—' Cantress started, and broke off sudden to throw up a hand. 'Shh!—*Listen!* She's comin'!'

Dim, far away, we heard the sound of the flyer.

'Watch it, now!' Cantress admonished. 'Hanley, take Charlie and Andrade and get across the track. We'll take her from both sides; that way, if there's any badges aboard her, we'll have 'em in a crossfire. But don't use your guns on a man 'less you have to.'

We waited till the three had got across the track.

Forlorn sound wailed from the engine. Up in the wind Tulare threw the switch bar. A red light shone from the steel tower over us. The semaphore waggled. Blinding light reached out and swept the tracks as the roaring monster hit the start of the bend.

There was a terrific screech as the brakes grabbed hold. The whole world shuddered. The ground lurched under us. The engine was past with a grinding squeal. The glow from the cab showed Cantress' white teeth locked in a grin as the great train slowed with a smell of hot iron fused against cold steel.

'*Now!*' Cantress said.

And, yanking our scarfs up over our noses, we went scrabbling up the shaley bank. Tulare

126

was running toward the glow of the engine. 'Ike!' Cantress shouted. 'Take Betsy with you an' go through the coaches!' He whirled and, with Corva, ran toward the express car.

Betsy caught at my arm. I saw the flash of her eyes in the light from the coaches. Eyes big and round, alarmed, asking guidance.

'Keep back in the shadows till we see how it's shaping.'

I threw a quick look toward the front of the train. Saw Tulare. He was herding the engine crew toward us.

I hopped up the steps of the nearest coach, shoved through the door and made my way forward through the panic-stricken passengers. Groans and oaths spiced the passengers' babel. A white faced drummer was bent forward in the aisle perspiringly stowing long green in his button shoes.

'Keep calm,' I said. 'You ain't goin' to be robbed,' and went out the door and into the next coach.

Windy Lipari was passing the hat. He must of seen by my eyes he was in the wrong pew. He let go the hat and grabbed for his cutter.

It was him or me. It wasn't going to be me. I tipped my gun snout and let him have it.

'Keep calm,' I told them, and backed out on the platform.

As I swung to the gravel, Trigger Hanley got off the next coach back of me. Andrade, with the light winking bright off his guns, leapt after

127

him.

'What was that shootin'?'

'Some fool tried to gun me.'

Right under my elbow Bronc Andrade's gun belched. A conductor, back yonder, had rushed into sight. He stood abruptly froze there, looking foolish, with nothing left of his lantern but a curved piece of wire and some shreds of bent metal.

With a sudden scared oath he dropped it and run.

It didn't look like we'd got much resistance.

There was somebody up a telegraph pole. He was cutting the wires.

I looked round for Betsy but couldn't see her.

Hanley said, 'C'mon. Let's get over—' and broke off as a man poked his head from the rear coach platform. Hanley lifted his gun. The luckless passenger let go his hold. He fell off the steps and rolled down the cinder bank.

Hanley punched the spent shells from his gun and reloaded.

There was a blur of figures by the door of the express car. I heard Cantress' voice snarling threats at the messenger.

We came up just as the man—finally moved by Cantress' talk of dynamite—rolled open the door. I saw him then by the light from his counter, his knees shaking as he put his hands up. Corva covered him with a rifle. Cantress told him to get down. Cantress and Hanley vaulted into the car.

I was about to follow when I heard a yell. Something bit past my cheek and ricocheted from the car. I spun just in time to see Bronc Andrade knock down a brakeman. He put three slugs through the man's prone body and then stepped over and kicked him brutally.

Hot breath made a sound as it come up out of me.

Andrade swung clear around with his gun snouts lifting.

'Thanks,' I said. 'You're sure mighty handy—at potting unarmed men.'

I shoved past his scowl and reached for the sack Hanley'd lugged to the door.

It was heavier than I'd thought. It slipped through my hands, hit the ground with a dull chink of metal.

Corva licked his lips and grinned.

CHAPTER EIGHTEEN

You got to have a flair for it to be a good train robber. Cantress' handling of the Texas Express was nothing to brag about. Luck was with him or we'd never got clear of it. Catch as catch can—a hell of a way to try robbing a railroad!

There was, for instance, that matter of Lipari, who'd been told to stay with the horses and who I'd caught with a gun going through the coaches. Time wasn't reckoned in the business at all; and there was too much blood—too much Texas, to put the thing plainly. Andrade and Hanley was too much cast after the pattern of Doolin; they were too excitable, too prone to gunplay.

I let go the sack and was ready to fetch another when a couple more guys got down off the train. They stood there, staring, by one of the coaches. I ain't never been sure, but I think they was train dicks. They reached for their pistols. The biggest guy fired.

Hanley's whiskers popped out of the car door. He let out a roar. I seen the glint of his lifting hardware. Him and Andrade both fired together.

The two fellows fell. You could tell, way they dropped, they wouldn't get up again.

'By God!' I said. 'Did you have to *kill* 'em?'

Hanley's round-flung stare was bright as an ax head. Cantress came to the door and heaved a couple of gunny sacks at me. 'Split the swag. We'll be leavin' directly.'

I was hotter'n a stamp iron, but I did like he said. I caught up the sacks and went over to the one I had dropped by Andrade—the one with the loot. I got out my skinning knife and bent down over it.

'Don't do it,' the messenger said. 'Don't cut that sack, boy.'

Andrade grabbed him. 'Button yore lip or

130

I'll rap yore skull for you!'

I cut the neck of the sack open. By the light of the coaches I could see what was in it. It was filled with cartwheels—new silver dollars, straight from the mint. In a couple of shakes we had it divided. Resacked. Tied. Ready to go.

Hanley jumped from the car with a mail sack. Cantress followed, hastily stuffing something inside his shirt.

But Corva had seen him. I saw Corva's eyes gleam. Tulare had seen it, too. He looked sullen. They figured he was holding out on them, I reckoned. They were probably right. That was the trouble with owlhooter outfits. Somebody was always holding out.

Cantress raked a look down the track. 'Who killed those passengers?'

'Hanley,' I said. 'Wanted to see 'em squirm.'

Cantress flung a black look at Hanley. But the Texan's look at me was blacker. Cantress wheeled, snapped an order at Corva: 'Herd the crew inside this car—shove the stiffs in there, too, an' put a wiggle in it.'

He put two fingers in his mouth and whistled.

The rest of our crowd came trotting up. All mounted. One of them had a bunch of led horses.

It come over me then I might of judged too hasty in figuring Lipari had disobeyed orders. He might of had orders I wasn't let in on. It struck me sudden there was a whole heap of things I hadn't been let in on.

We unlimbered our guns and tore off like a twister.

*　　*　　*

As we rode through the brightening light of dawn the gang was boisterous about our haul. Two sacks of silver to be explored and divided. Their spirits was high as their greed built pictures of what they would do when their shares was given them. Tulare allowed he'd be going into business. Two or three talked high of a trip to the Argentine. Andrade was going to buy him a hooker joint. I reckoned the most of them would spend it on likker.

The hollow in which we had waited the train angled sharp southwest a mile farther on. I knew it because we had come that way. I wondered where was the draw Hanley'd left the preacher in.

Thought of the preacher brought up thoughts of Betsy . . . I was shocked to realize in the rush of events I had all but forgot her. It didn't seem possible a man could forget—

With my cheeks firing up I sent a look round me. Bet wasn't with us!

I looked again.

I was right the first time.

But now a further awareness grabbed me.

The pulse of my blood jumped frantic with

tumult.

There were other shapes missing. Hanley's, C—

With the goosebumps crawling my spine I shouted: *'Cantress!* Hold up! Hold up a second!'

But my wits had come too late to the rescue. Too late.

We were rounding the bend.

From the gulch's crumbling rims, from the rocks of its floor, flame licked at us in livid streaks. There must of been near a dozen rifles pouring their lethal cargo at us. Lead shrilled through our ranks like hail. From out of the rocks and tangled chaparral, asleep so recent in the peace of centuries, leaped howling monsters, wild shouting and firing. Grotesque shapes, sprung whole from nightmares. Hooded faces and flapping blankets. Through the ragged smoke of their rifles they loomed—demons from hell come rushing us madly.

Cantress stood stiff, stood taut in his stirrups, dark face set in the bleakness of sculpture. I seen his eyes gleam hate and fury. Saw him snatch the gun from his scabbarded hip. Saw the white flame belch from its snout like lightning.

Then the howling shapes was into us, at us. All was resolved in a racketing clamor, in the screech and wail of continous gunfire. Some man's high yell slashed weirdly through it. Some fellow beside me grunted and vanished.

133

A horse come rocketing into me—reared. From the off side something bludgeoned my shoulder; come near blasting me out of the saddle. I grabbed the horn. With my free hand, slammed three slugs square into that climbing bronc's belly. It squealed like a damn sawmill whistle.

'*Damn you! Damn you!*' Cantress was shouting.

But I hadn't no time to look for Cantress. It was up to him to look out for himself.

I come aware my gun was clicking on empties. I heaved the thing at a hooded face and yanked my rifle from under the fender. Some barrel-toned fool kept shouting and shouting. It was quite a spell before I knew it was me.

I shut my mouth and dug in the spurs for a rocky out-cropping off to the left. There was another guy rushing the same way, frantic. Our horses collided—sent him flying. It pleasured me plenty to see it was Corva.

I made the outcrop and flung my saddle. Whirled. Quartered back to the handiest crevice and thrust my carbine across its shoulder. I shot to drop them.

My lead found targets. A bay broke stride and come apart, flinging its rider like a stone from a slingshot. A seraped horseman, throwing down on Cantress, folded over his pommel with a fading cry. My third shot skittered off a lifting rifle. After that I had to quit looking for a spell.

But soon as the drum of lead slacked off and the last ricochet went screeching skyward, I cuffed off my hat and looked again. There was two guys faced in my direction, stuffing fresh shells in their heated smoke poles.

The nearest guy straightened and I seen his eyes glint. I levered another load to its seat. I tipped the muzzle and let him have it. He jackknifed forward with both hands digging at his darkening shirtfront.

The other man was lucky. A snorting, pitching, riderless bronc cut across my sights as I squeezed the trigger. The horse went down. The man got away in the churning dust.

As I wiped the sweat from my eyes and reloaded, a quick burst of firing to the left and below me lifted hammering layers of sound through the gulch. Cantress was shouting oaths in a frenzy; he was lost in a tangle of milling shapes I could only half see in the alkaline dust fog. I steadied the carbine's barrel and waited.

Out of the dust come a long, high cry. Guns beat up the echoes again. I was straining forward, trying to make some sense of the gyrating scene, when a dead branch sharply cracked behind me.

It was close, of course, else I'd not of heard it through that dinning uproar. Twisting, half ducking, I slammed around.

I hadn't no chance to use my carbine.

I hadn't no chance at all—not a particle.

There was a guy right behind me. A long geared shape with the red sun dripping off his shoulders; off the flour sack hood that covered his features. His left hand was wrapped about a lifted gunstock.

I saw that much—saw the ring on his finger—saw the limp as he leaped.

The world exploded in a million stars.

CHAPTER NINETEEN

I was being stomped—you couldn't tell me different. They had turned an outlaw bronc loose on me. Some fool was fanning it with his Stet hat. I could hear the buffeting slaps of it hit him.

Every inch of me howled its protest.

You'd howl, too, if a bronc was stomping you!

Pain ripped me, slogged me, pummeled and pounded me till I couldn't tell up from down or sideways.

It was mostly my head; but the belly, too, was being pounded out of me.

I yelled like hell, trying to tell them to quit it. But there wasn't no sound come out of my mouth.

It come to me finally my tongue wasn't working; it was swole, jammed tight against the roof of my mouth.

Damn queer, I thought. Hadn't never been that way before, didn't seem like. The sides of my mouth was aching some, too.

Then I got it. I mean, I seen how it was I'd corraled all them miseries. Some kind soul had stuffed a gag in my mouth; and I'd been tied face down, knotted meal sack fashion, across the back of a bronc that some damn fool had left the saddle onto. It was that saddle was jolting a hole through my navel. That was when I remembered Flour Sack, and the lick he had fetched me with the steel of his gun barrel.

But a heap of my other rememberings was worse. Like the discovery I'd made about Bet's disappearance—and about Charlie, too. Where the hell had they gone to? And where was that whiskered Texan off at. Were they all three together like they'd come to the robbing?

It was funny, I thought, nobody'd seen them fade.

Then I got a worse thought. Maybe somebody *had*! Maybe it was all part and parcel of some slick scheme devolved by the sly, crafty mind of Ed Cantress. Maybe Charlie's got wind of Ed's prospective nuptials, and had opened his jaw just a little too far.

It would be like him, I thought. He was brash as a hatter.

Or Betsy, just possible, had told him how

things was. She might of. She'd told *me*.

A yarn like that would churn Charlie considerable. He was young and romantic. Couldn't tolerate injustice. Look how he'd took up for me against Hanley—

By grab! Could *that* be back of it? Could Hanley have changed his damned mind about Charlie? One thing was certain: I'd been grabbed by Sundance.

Sure I'd been wanting to come up with him. Sure! But not hogtied to the back of no bronc!

I knew one thing. It was Sundance, all right, who had rapped my head for me. I'd heard aplenty about that jasper. About his limp and his hood and his southpaw gunplay.

There were just two things that might work to my favor—just two skinny chances my luck might come in again. The note I'd sent Tilghman, and the weight I was leaning on Charlie Kaintuck.

It could be that Tilghman, working on the note I'd sent him by Betsy, would get to wondering what the devil had happened to me. A heap more probable was my cherished thought that, by this time, he was bound to be dogging the trail of the train robbers. I hadn't seen nobody trying to hide it.

The other possibility might prove a mixed blessing, but it had got to the point where I'd got to have help; and there was no help handy unless I made out to use Charlie.

Such being the case, I had put a few chips

on him. I'd given him the pig-sticker to hold for safekeeping. And had told him a few things—not nothing important; just a few hints, kind of. I had mentioned the dubious pleasures of owlhooting, then had sourly disparaged them by what it would get you. I had mentioned the Daltons, the Youngers and Jameses. I told him how Sam Bass had died at the hands of the Texas Rangers. Of how Pat Garrett had trapped Bill Bonney; of Curly Bill's finish, and the death of Zwing Hunt.

I wasn't forgetting that star-packer talk, but I reckoned such talk for a kid's bravado. I had sounded him pretty careful, I figured, and the results hadn't changed my notion. He had showed me, kind of sheepish like, a much read letter his folks had sent him—'Come home, son. We had almost sooner know you was dead than think of you carousing with thieves and killers.' It was easy to see he was just a fool kid—just another such sprout as Russian Bill and the hosts of others who had colored too rosy the west's wooly ways.

So I'd give him the knife to keep care of for me. A guiding hand was what he needed; someone to steady the reins a bit for him. 'String along with me,' I told him gruffly, 'and I'll show you something that's a heap more excitin' than larrupin' round like a chicken with its head off; somethin' considerable more fittin' to a growed man's notions than stickin' up banks an' runnin' off cattle.'

139

He'd give me a odd look, putting that knife away. Trying to savvy, I reckon, what the hell I was up to. But I wasn't telling him yet.

Before I talked I'd got to give him reason to be disgusted with bad men. I'd got to show this crowd up for sorry sports, for tinhorn skunks and belly-crawling sidewinders. There was one other way I might convince him. Charlie figured Trigger Hanley was big-bore hardware, a real he-smokeroo from who-bit-the-bolts-off. If I could show Hanley up . . .

Trouble was now I wasn't in no shape to show up nobody. I didn't know where Hanley was, nor even Charlie. I didn't know where I was myself, even. And if Charlie had cut and run for it—or if Hanley'd decided he couldn't count on him, I'd be out the kid's help and the damn knife likewise.

It was then I noticed the bronc I was tied on.

All I could see was a part of one leg and the critter's belly. But that was aplenty, now I put my mind to it.

A mouse-colored roan. I hadn't never seen but one colored like it. That one was Hanley's.

Hanley! The guy to which Ed had so recent remarked, 'Strikes me uncommon odd, Hair-Trigger, that you and Sundance both limp and are leftpaws.'

The shock of that memory run down to my bootsoles.

The horses stopped.

'Cut him loose,' Cantress said. 'We're going to settle this now.'

Cantress!

I never rightly wondered what it was they was going to settle. I was a heap too busy congratulating my luck I was still with the Cantress outfit. All this time I'd been plumb certain it was Sundance Kid had grabbed me. Sundance—which was just another name for Hanley!

When they cut the ropes I hadn't no more control of myself than a meal sack. A couple of guys eased me down, helped me straighten. One of them pulled the gag from my mouth. I had no more strength than if my blood was water.

Andrade, Hanley and Cantress come up.

I sure wasn't glad to see that Texan. If what I figured was right, it was that whiskered devil that had showed them stars to me.

Cantress opened things up with a question. 'What have you got to say for yourself?'

It took me quite a spell to say anything. My mouth felt like a bundle of burlap somebody dragged through the dust with a rope.

'What the hell,' Andrade sneered, 'do you expect him to say? What *can* he say? We got the deadwood on that stinker *this* time!'

But Cantress said to Hanley, quiet:

'Suppose you tell your way of it, Trigger.'

'About in the middle of thet shootin',' he said, 'I seen this buck light out fo' a rock pile. The Mex was reinin' thet way, likewise. Mister Stroud heah, seh, rapped him one with his smoke pole an', whiles he was reelin', shot him outa the saddle. Killed 'im jes' like you'd gut-shoot a wolf!'

'That's a—'

'You can do your talking after he's finished.'

I buttoned my lip. Cantress' eyes wasn't pleasant.

'When we got behind them rocks,' Hanley growled, 'he commenced layin' round with thet .45–90. I don't say he done it—don't say he killed 'em; but you all know how many men we lost—an' the's some more o' us heah ain't feelin' too frisky.'

He looked round and spat. '*Somebody* shot 'em.'

It was a wonder I kept hold of my temper. Looked like all of my troubles went back to this Texan. I was mightily tempted to tell him a few; but just in time I recollected that flour sack.

I said, 'Finished, have you?'

'*No*, I ain't finished!' Hanley yelled in a passion. 'I ain't *begun*! Time I git finished, seh, this gang'll be rid o' you!

'Been a deal o' talk of spies in this outfit. Been a passle of leaks in the plans we've hatched late like. Cantress,' he said, ramping

142

sly eyes around, 'hez been allowin' ouah leak is a felleh named Charlie.'

'*Me?*' Charlie said with his cheeks roiling up. You could see he was mad, half mad and half flustered.

'Neveh mind,' Hanley grinned, looking round plenty sly like, 'I we'n't neveh the kind to swalleh such flipflop. When I see rattleweed I reckon to know it. This scound'el—' he pawed up his whiskers and squinched his eyes baleful, '—this poison vipeh the chief hez been coddlin', hez been knowed to me fo' a right smaht while. We've met befo'. In N' Mexico Territory. Some o' you gents, if you'd knowed what I know, would of been hell-rarin' t' spill yo' guts.

'But thet ain't my way. When I fix t' call a man, I figgeh to have ev'y last bet coppered— I'd of had 'im las' night if thet gal hadn't gone back on me.'

'You can leave Miz' O'Daye out of—'

'That's as may be,' Hanley rumbled. 'Time to've done that was befo' you hooked up with her. I told you that but you wouldn't listen. Thet's been yo' trouble—you don't *neveh* listen. All you care about's yo' Cantress pride. *Pride!*'

He spat and said harshly: 'Yo' goddam pride cost us fo' men las' night!'

A wild, headlong fury caught Cantress' cheeks—caught them and twisted them, crouching him ugly.

Hanley laughed in his face. 'Put a valve on yo' whistle; I ain't done yet. This slick talkin' One-Shot you're so all-fi-ehed sot on is a Fo't Smith depity, name o' Ike Stroud. An' if thet ain't enough, he's likewise yo' nemesis—that goddam Sundance you been howlin' about!'

'Sundance!' Cantress' jaw dropped.

You could see the sick color that was greening his cheeks, the sicker confusion that was tangling his mind.

Hanley chortled.

'How else did you figgeh he c'ld know so damn much?'

'But Sundance—'

'The' ain't no buts to it! Ask 'im what was he doin' by yo' windeh the otheh night. Ask 'im what he was doin' watchin' you an' thet O'Daye gal when you was tryin' t' spahk her out in the brush thet same evenin'! You pore fool! *She's* been his spy till he come heah in pe'son! Look at his face if you don't want t' believe me!'

I pulled loose of Charlie and the other guy holding me. The rage his lies had boiled up in me—the brass-plated gall of him calling me Sundance, had burned out the last sign of caution in me. I knew the scabbard on my hip was empty; but that wasn't stopping me—I sprang at him anyway. I planted four knuckles right betwixt his damn eyes. Another four took him under the chin and went off like the sound of a board banging water.

144

I smacked him again as he staggered back, reeling. Then the gang climbed over me like a ton of dropped earth. Stopped me, smothered me, just with the weight of them—tromped me and stomped me, drove all the breath out of me. When they yanked me up I guessed I was done for.

But luck had come back in the shape of Ed Cantress. It was Cantress' pride that turned the tables for me.

'Get back, you fools! Let loose of him— hear me? Get back, you wolves; *I'm* runnin' this crew!'

Before the threat of his eyes—of those guns snouts, the gang fell back; left me standing free.

'Heel yourself,' he said. 'Get that Texan's pistols . . . Fine! We'll see how far he'll pack his lies now!'

His eyes blazed at Hanley. 'Get up on your haunches, you fork-tongued polecat. We've listened to your ranting; now we'll look at your proof.'

Tulare bent over and helped Hanley up. There was an insane glitter in the Texan's eyes as he reached to his leathers and found their sheaths empty.

There was a beading of sweat standing out round his whiskers. But there wasn't no cringing about him—not none. He stood with burly shoulders squared truculent; gave back Cantress' hate with a curdling malevolence.

145

A nasty suspicion got to churning my mind.

Cantress said: 'What was your idea claiming Ike was Sundance?'

'As the boys can tell you,' Hanley growled, 'I had dropped back a piece to git a stone outa the frog of my bronc's hind foot—jes' befo' the fight opened up, thet was. When I come bustin' up I seen this friend of yorn bashin' Corva; shootin' him outa the saddle. Then he cut an' run f' thet rock pile I mentioned.

'I cut fer it, too; worked around behind it. He'd jes' emptied his carbine into our crowd an' was takin' a flour sack from his pocket—'

'That's a goddam lie!'

I was starting for him when Cantress said: 'Go on. Let's have the rest of it.'

'Jes' as he started t' put the thing on, a branch snapped under my foot an' he seen me, He re'ched fo' his cutteh, but I was too quick for him. I brought my gun barrel down on his haid—look 'im oveh 'f you don't like my say-so. Where d'you spose thet dried blood come from? A gun barrel whack ain't so easy got rid of you can't find the place if you want t' look fo' it.'

He puffed out his breath and eyed me malignant.

'Told you I never jumped no man without I could prove—'

'Come you're so handy with proof,' Cantress said, 'where's the flour sack?'

'Right heah!' Hanley grinned, and pulled it

146

out of his pocket.

*   *   *

I was goddam glad I'd given Charlie the knife.

Neither pride nor outraged vanity, nor all the white hot fury roused in Cantress by Hanley's insults, could scour away such proof as that.

Doubt edged the scowl filming Cantress' cheekbones. It was a cinch I'd soon be peeled for a searching.

And the hell of it was, I still had my badge.

A search would disclose it.

I took a quick look around, trying to figure my chances. They wasn't of a nature to inspire such confidence. Charlie's look was bleak; he was watching me nervous. Distrust and suspicion shaped the other men's faces.

'Ask him,' says Hanley, 'if his name ain't Stroud.'

'Sure is Stroud,' I said. 'Have I ever denied it?'

Malice was a leer in the Texan's eyeballs. 'Let's heah him deny packin' tin fo' Heck Thomas—'

'If that's the best you can do . . .' I looked at him scornful. I said to the others: 'I'm sure learnin' a heap, rubbin' elbows with you guys. Of all the untrustin', back-bitin' lobos—'

'That ain't answering the question—'

'This will,' I said. 'I worked under Heck for

147

goin' on five years—an' would still be ridin' with him, like enough, if I hadn't been treated like a blanket-wrapped Injun.'

The bunch got so quiet you could hear the damned crickets.

'So what?' I said. 'Whyn't you ask what the rest of this bunch was doin' 'fore they backslid into bein' renegade owlhooters? For all *you* know, mebbe they was *all* star packers! Mebbe they got plumb fed up, same as me, with the damn red tape an' the—'

Tulare said, soft like: 'You allowin' you ain't still workin' for them butchers?'

'You reckon I'd be round here if I *was* workin' for 'em? You reckon I'd of stuck up the Buckhorn Saloon? Spiced that up with horse stealin' an' then, for good measure, helped you hold up that train? Them things sound like a star packer's habits? Would a hard workin' tinbadge go out of his way to gun a man that was tippin' off Tilghman where this bunch was holed up at?'

'We don't know,' he smiled, 'that's the reason you blasted him. *Might* of been the other way round. Might of been Benson seen *you* comin' out of Bill's office. All *we've* got is your word for it—'

'You undertakin' to call me a liar?'

'Not me,' he said, 'I'm reservin' my judgment.'

'By Gawd,' I said, looking hard at Cantress, 'it's a wonder to me, with this breed of dogs,

148

Fort Smith ain't had you danglin' long ago! I'd sooner herd with wild snakes—'

'That kinda gab ain't buyin' you nothin',' one of the Hanley crowd growled. 'Take more than talk t' git your tail outa *this* crack—'

'My tail' I told him, 'ain't in no crack.'

'Ask the hard guy,' Andrade said with a sneer, 'what he's done with the loot he took off of them coaches.'

I could feel the smash of their bright, hard stares.

This was it, I thought. This was what they'd been waiting for.

It was Cantress' quiet tones busted the silence.

'Just a second,' he said. 'This wrangle brings out one thing that's been needing settling for the last couple weeks. The reason we been having such a run of hard luck is the hit-or-miss fashion this gang's been organized. You banded together and elected me boss. But there's a lot of you fellows would rather have Hanley.'

He looked them over, seeing how his words had roughed up their faces. 'I don't give a damn whether I'm boss or not, but if I am, by God, you're going to take my orders. You can't run a outfit with more than one boss. It might be Hanley'd make a better boss than I been— lot of you boys seem to be of that notion.

'It's all right with me. I don't hold hard feelings. But make up your minds. Make 'em up now. Hanley's a fighter—a ring-tailed roarer when it comes to gunplay. He's brash and headlong and likewise a schemer; likes nothing better than to see a gent kicking with a slug through his gizzard. If that's the kind of fellow you want then give him my job. You'll find him sharp and suspicious, swift to pick quarrels; quick to sense failings, quick to smell out a traitor. You'll find him given to making his own rules and making you like them. He's got no use for either women or whiskey—told me just the other night if he had his way there'd not be either of them round our hideout.

'But that's all right with me,' Cantress said; and his tones was flat as the prairie miles. 'You boys are the ones to be suited. If that's what you want I'll not stand in your way. Arbitration's my method. The vote of the majority.

'You that figure Hanley stands for the things you want should rightly vote for him to be bossing things. He says he don't want to boss things. But he won't work with me, won't sit in my confab, goes against every man I put any confidence in. I won't say a word against him; I won't condemn him for slipping off nights on raids of his own, nor for the extra privileges he takes to himself—I'll not even ask how much swag his tricks net him, nor how many friends he figures to count on.

'I don't *give* a damn. But from here on out,

150

if I'm to be boss, Mister Hanley and his cronies is going to take my orders and carry them out to the last damn letter! If you like his ways better than mine, name him boss. Now's the time. All you fellows that want Hanley for chief just step right out and shove up your hands.'

Both Andrade's fists went above his head promptly.

The Texan, grinning, wheeled to look round.

The grin turned thin on his lips and froze.

The only hands showing belonged to Bronc Andrade.

CHAPTER TWENTY

Hanley's smile licked tight and vanished. White-cheeked, Bronc Andrade lowered his arms and backed two steps toward the edge of the circle. His spurs clanked harsh in the sudden quiet.

'There's your gang,' Cantress said; and some fool snickered.

He was wheeling away when Cantress said, 'Just a moment, Trigger. We'll eat the whole rabbit while we're at it. Like I said, I'm not the man to hang onto a grudge; you're welcome to stay, if you're so inclined, but there are a number of things I want put in the record. You

151

been layin' for me for a long time, mister—been playing the oldest game in the world; you even went so far as to look into my past, into what I had done before I showed up here. If you wanted me out of the way so bad, why have you wasted your time hatching up schemes when you could have dragged your guns and wound me up long ago?'

Hanley said in a gruff, choked voice, 'You've got me all wrong, seh. I never wanted you out of the way. You've proved it yo'se'f—if I had I'd of gunned you.'

'Would you, Trigger? I wonder,' said Cantress with a cool, dry smile. 'I'm wondering if it wasn't that notion that prompted you to look into my past; if it wasn't the things you dug out of my past that decided you scheming might prove a heap cheaper?'

'What we stopped here to settle,' growled Andrade testily, 'was what we should do with this damn spy!'

'What do *you* think we ought to do with him, Andrade?'

'That's up to you—you're top screw of this outfit.'

'Not sure I'm convinced he's a spy,' Cantress murmured. 'Not sure!'

Andrade stared incredulous. 'After what Trigger just got done tellin' us?'

'There's a faint idea in my mind,' Cantress said, 'that Trigger's telling might—ummm—be a little prejudiced. He doesn't like Ike—'

'You can't get around that flour sack hood!'

'Your judgment's a little inclined to be hasty. And you don't like Ike any better than Trigger does.' Cantress said, cool and easy: 'It's in my mind that sack may belong to Trigger.'

'You accusin' *me* of bein' Sundance?'

'You don't have to shout, Trigger,' Cantress smiled. 'I'm not accusing anybody. I'm just pointing out that you had the sack. You also limp, just the same as Sundance. You use your left hand more than you do your right and you spend a heap of your time out of camp. I reckon we'll hear Ike's side of the story.'

'The lyin' word of a sneakin' tinbadge!'

'Ike's ridin' with us. It's not a man's past but what is is *now* that concerns this outfit. Weren't you packing a star once yourself? Weren't you the fellow used to marshal San Saba?'

Hanley glared, clamped his mouth shut.

'Well, Ike,' Cantress said. 'Suppose you give us your side of the story.'

So I told them how it happened Corva'd fell from his saddle. How I'd made it back of that pile of boulders and begun throwing down on Sundance's masked raiders. How I'd heard that branch crack back of me and whirled to find a guy in a flour sack bringing his gun barrel down on my cranium. 'If it wasn't Hanley,' I said, cocked for trouble, 'how'd he know about that damn branch crackin'?'

153

Cantress said 'Ummm.' Looked from one to the other of us.

The whiskered Texan sneered.

'You wouldn't of said nothin' about thet branch if—'

'Damn right he wouldn't!' Andrade shouted. 'Ask 'im what he did with the loot from them coaches! What'd he do with that sack of silver? Who'd he shoot in that coach 'fore jumpin' out? Where's Lipari—'

'I ain't Lipari's keeper,' I said. 'An' I told you about that shot in the coach—some nervous fool tried to bring up his cutter. As for the loot and the silver, Sundance—'

'Yeah! Sundance! Mebbe you better fork over them guns—'

*　　*　　*

'*I'll* give the orders,' Cantress' voice reminded.

'Then by Gawd,' Andrade gritted, 'you better start givin' them! Give an order to search him!'

I seen old Four Eyes watching me sly-like; I reckoned he was thinking about that knife. I'd got considerable thought from it, likewise; but, mostly, my thoughts was of that badge I was packing. Of what would follow when they found it on me.

'Go ahead!' I growled, making to put the best face I could on it. There was the barest chance, if I showed to be willing, they'd maybe

154

decide I'd got nothing worth finding.

I needn't of fretted. Not then, anyway. Cantress' head was taking care of everything. 'Toss Hanley back his hoglegs, Ike. He might take cold being naked that way. We'll go back to the canyon. Time we get there I'll have this figured.'

I give the Texan back his pistols. I got to thinking of the dead men back of us, wondering if anybody'd thought to bury them. Fierce critters roved the wastes of this country, slinking things that lived on carrion.

*   *   *

We were back again where we'd started from. Back between the red walls of Sundance Canyon. I was still free and able, but without no weapons, a poor shorn lamb surrounded by buzzards. And it wasn't no comfort to reflect on the number of times I'd decided to get out of there.

Hanley and his bootstrapping friends were outvoted—outgeneraled, but they hadn't give up their intention of searching me.

I reckoned they had Cantress' knife on their minds.

If it had been just the knife I'd laugh in their faces. But I knew, if they searched me, they'd turn up my badge. I had it cached in my boot where I couldn't get at it.

All the way back Hanley'd rode his nag like

a guy with lockjaw. But Andrade got in plenty of chin wagging. I'd seen him talking to half a dozen fellows, muttering down under his breath and throwing me scowls with every sixth word or so.

Where I'd made my mistake was in not clearing out when I'd had the chance—that time I'd gone in to Perry, for instance. Instead of making for Tilghman's office that day, I'd of done a sight better if I'd pulled my freight. I could have got in touch with Tilghman from Guthrie. It was a little bit late to be thinking of that though.

I was sure in my own mind that that whiskered Texan was Sundance Kid. But, unless I could mighty quick convince Ed Cantress, it looked like Ike Stroud's hours was numbered.

My only chance, aside from that, was the swift arrival of Bill Tilghman with a posse.

I got to counting up time. In that note I'd give Betsy before we'd left camp last night, I'd told Bill how to get out here and the approximate strength of Cantress' outfit. I'd also mentioned what little I knew of Doolin's plan for Ingalls. Betsy would just about have had time to get Bill that note before Hanley and Charlie had fetched her to the train robbery. Probably slipped it under his door, I figured. Before he could have made up his mind whether or not he could put any faith in it, word would have reached him about the

Texas Express. It was plain what he'd take for his obvious duty; he'd have sworn in a posse and took after the robbers.

Bill would be coming along any minute— perhaps he was out there now, surrounding us. Trapped in this pocket they would make short work of us . . .

That was when I remembered our brush with Sundance.

My soaring spirits come down like froze water.

With all that maze of crisscrossed tracks, there wasn't nobody breathing could of said with luck which crowd had made this, or which had made that one. Only thing Bill could do was to follow each one up.

I said goodbye to any luck from Tilghman.

And right on the heels of that tough parting I caught two words out of Andrade's pipe laying.

Law wagon!

Them words jerked me up like a three-eights rope.

I didn't have to hear any more words out of him. It wasn't the knife they was figuring to hunt for. They knew well enough I didn't have that knife. They knew mighty well what I *was* packing, though.

That Fort Smith badge!

What a loon I had been not to've guessed it sooner. First thing Hanley'd have done, would been search me. Quick as that gun barrel had batted me down he'd have gone through my clothing from shirt neck to sock feet—he'd been hunting for that knife like a dog after cow ticks.

So he couldn't of missed getting a look at my badge.

If I'd had a gun I'd of cut and run for it.

But I hadn't no gun. I'd lost mine in that brush with Sundance. And Cantress had made me give back Hanley's pistols.

So here I was, back in camp once more.

With a plenty of prospects—all of them bad.

CHAPTER TWENTY-ONE

The sun was down, and the men were getting so edgy you could taste it almost, when the shod hoof of an oncoming horseman came racketing down off the gulch's red walls.

It was the mealsack of Old Man O'Daye that rode into the flare of the rekindled cook fire. He pulled up with a wheeze and grunted testily as he groaned his weight down out of the saddle. You'd think to listen at him, he had packed the horse, instead of it being the other way round.

He scowled, rasping a hand across his unshaved jaw. 'One of you fellers—' he began, and stopped. Stiffening, he slowly turned, peering puzzled and nervous at the fire-stained faces. He was a coyote, suddenly sensing danger.

Cantress, coming into the light, paused, and then planted a fist into O'Daye's face—hard.

'You miserable tickbird!' he flung at him, bitter. 'Ain't I told you a hundred times not to come out here? *Ain't* I?'

O'Daye tried to swallow. He gagged and fidgeted. He cringed away from Ed, licking his lips; jerked a hand up, whimpering, to the ache in his face, brought it down, out before him, splashed with red and shaking.

'What you been up to, anyway, damn you? Trying to sell us out to that fool, Bill Tilghman?'

Cantress, impatient, caught his shoulder and shook him. 'Speak up, Damn you! Talk— 'fore I drag it out of you!'

'B—Bill ain't in town—he's off someplace in the hills with a posse. Somethin' t' do with that feller, Doolin. Doolin's wild bunch come in an' raided Perry las' night—cleaned out the Buckhorn an' the stage office—struck straight north like a shuck in a twister.'

'You ride out here to tell me *that*?'

The demand in Cantress' tone was intolerant.

'No—No, I . . . I come out here 'cause—'

His voice squeaked, scared like. He backed away a few steps, licked his lips and blurted: ' 'Cause I gotta see Betsy! I—'

'Damn you!' Cantress snarled, stepping

159

after him. 'What the hell you fixing to pull? You know dawn well the girl's not here—'

'Not here!'

O'Daye, in mid flight, stopped, incredulous. He stood there gaping at Cantress stupidly. 'No—not here, you say?'

A look, like doubt, crossed the gun boss' features. He lowered his fist; eyed the man intently. 'You meaning to tell me she's not in town?'

'She *must* be here,' O'Daye mumbled hoarsely. 'Your men come in an'—'

Charlie's drawl, from the shadows, sliced across his talk. 'I took her home again after that. After we held up the Texas Flyer.'

Hanley sprang to his feet with a ripped-out oath. *'Took her home!'* he shouted. 'Took her *home*? After—'

'Well, practically,' Charlie said, a little worried. 'I took her far as—'

'After what we caught her up to. You damn fool!' Hanley snarled at him, wicked. 'Ed—' he said, whipping round on Cantress, 'I ain't had time t' mention this sooneh, but we caught yo' wife comin' outa Bill's office. When we went to fecth 'er fo' thet train robbin' dido. Caught 'er right on the po'ch o' Bill Tilghman's office! What do you think she had in her fist? A note, By Gawd! A note t' Bill f'om this two-faced sidewindeh yo' so all-fi'ed proud of!'

I couldn't say nothing.

The Texan's blast left me dumb as a fence

post.

The whole gang was eyeing me.

The silence piled up like the blocks in a ice house.

I knew I was done for. But I wasn't thinking of that. I don't guess, really, I was thinking of anything. I couldn't take in so much grief all to once.

Betsy . . . It didn't seem possible. I could still feel her arms like she'd clamped them around me; the soft, throbbing curves of her warm, eager body—

And all the time she'd been married to Cantress!

Rage tore through me as I thought how she'd tricked me. Used the woman's lure of her to prove me a sucker. Took the note I had give her and run straight to Hanley.

No wonder she'd been wanting me to gun Ed Cantress!

It was *Hanley* she wanted—she'd made up to me so I'd rid her of Cantress! So I'd do for that Texan what he hadn't the gumption to do for himself!

I wasn't deceived none by the way he put it. I wasn't swallowing that 'Caught' stuff noways. Caught—*hell!* If that had been so . . . *Christ's blood!* Nobody connected with the owlhooter breed would go round flourishing a note to a lawman. She'd *give* him that note, that's what she had done—gone hunting him, damn her, and give it straight over to him!

Charlie's voice, thin and high, scratched across the silence. 'We don't know Ike wrote it . . . You're just—'

'We kin damn quick prove it!' Hanley shouted. *'Grab 'im!'*

'Damn right!' Andrade leered; and I seen the fire-glint dance off his pistol—heard the gang's sullen growls like the cry of a wolf pack as they come leaping toward me.

'Seach the varmint!'

'Strip him!'

'Kill 'im!'

'Get a rope!' someone shouted.

I saw them pile up, staring. Saw them blink and goggle like they couldn't believe what their own eyes told them. That Cantress was still of a mind to stand by me.

I couldn't believe it myself. Not hardly.

But there he was. Standing square alongside me. Holding them back with the look of his eyes.

I found myself searching the cheeks of him, curious seeking; to find what these other men knew of him, what danger was hid behind his arrogance.

His lips curled thinly as he looked them over. 'I'm still plenty able to give out the orders—'

'Then give 'em!' rasped Hanley.

Cantress drawled, 'I aim to,' and a chilled, tight stillness shut down round us.

Gleams from the fire stained the taut, ugly

162

faces. Violence was a smell in the air around us. Andrade lifted a hand and pointed. 'See that feller, O'Daye? Take a good, long squint at him. Know 'im, don't you?'

The old man's blowsy cheeks changed color. 'By Gawd, I do!' His E-string voice twanged shrill, excited. 'He's a stinkin' star packer!'

'Hear that?' Andrade said with his eyes aglitter.

There was a silent laughter on Cantress' lips.

'A tickbird's word!' he drawled, coldly scornful. 'Tim O'Daye's Christian qualities should endear him to you; a fine, large hog, getting fat on the sweat of his betters.'

'Gawd's gullet!' O'Daye bleated. 'Is that any way t' talk about your friends? If it wasn't fer me—'

'Yeah. I know that by heart. I can recite it backwards,' Cantress scoffed. 'You and your kind to sound the alarm, to bring information, to lend us money and food when we're down and out, starving; to give us aid and shelter when we're hunted and hurt—all for a nice fat profit, mind you. When the profit don't come up to what the law's offering, you'll turn us in just as smug and virtuous! D'you suppose,' he scowled, with a look at Hanley, 'I place any trust in the word of such parasites?'

'Hell's fire!' Hanley shouted. 'I'm *tellin'* you, ain't I? All you got to do is search—'

'I'm not searching no man on a tickbird's

163

say so.'

You could see the clash of their eyes in the fireglow.

It was a matter of face—a contest of wills. You could see by their looks how the gang was shifting; the odds slithering over to Hanley. It was dog eat dog—the law of the lost lands. Because his pride wouldn't let him admit Hanley right—not even in the face of the man's piled up evidence—Cantress was losing his hold on these men.

Hanley's face showed flushed and rageful but there was jubliant triumph in the flash of his stare. He said in a high, half-strangled voice: 'You *refuse?*' and the hush turned lurid with the savage gleam of the men's judging eyes.

In that quiet I could hear the rasp of their breathing; could see the implications unleashed by Hanley threading their cheeks with a look of fury. In about two seconds, I told myself, all hell was going to be loosed on cart wheels.

I had no weapon—no more chance than a cricket. I cocked my muscles for a flying leap at the reins of the storekeeper's jaded horse. I cocked them, I say.

But I made no leap.

CHAPTER TWENTY-TWO

Pride was the key to Cantress' character. More and more I could see it was the key to his actions. He was bad from choice. It was his bid for attention. He was like to get plenty of attention now.

Hanley'd played this slick. Got us wedged hard and fast in the crotch of his craft. It looked pretty much like we'd heard our last owl hoot.

But me and the Texan both figured wrong.

It took Cantress' grin to open my eyes.

Like a bolt from the blue then I seen what he'd done; over-played his hand, over-reached himself badly. In his tempestuous rush to be finally rid of us he had stacked the cards too steep for his purpose; he had failed to allow for the height of Ed's ego, had made it impossible for the man to back down.

I had a wild hope then. If I saw this thing right, it would not be compatible with Cantress' pride to save himself and let them have me. To save his face he had got to save both of us.

I sneaked a look at him. Saw the rash grin tightening the skin round his cheekbones. There was a gleam in his eyes that was brighter than gun steel.

He was smart. He'd been figuring. He'd

been a mile ahead of this gang all the way. He'd remembered something Hanley'd forgotten; that in every crowd—every mob, if you will—there was just one man whose shouted word or lifted hand could set things off, could get hell started.

I seen him turning; saw his glance rake round till his eyes found Andrade. I knew right off he had picked the man. It wouldn't be the whiskered Texan, because Hanley was cast in the gun boss pattern that, given half a chance, always delegates violence.

It was plain he had planned to delegate it now; but Cantress moved a little too quick for him. He wasn't quite ready when Cantress said: 'Andrade! Get your junk and get out of here.'

I saw the gang's mouths come popping open. They were caught off balance by the unexpected; he had rung in a change that hadn't been allowed for, upsetting the whole range of Hanley's plotting. Andrade, waiting for his cue, was caught flatfooted, completely unprepared. There had been no provision in Hanley's plans for this and Andrade, a leather slapper, was not of a caliber for such fast thinking. He stood scowling and hesitant, the gleam of his eyes holding baffled wonderment, the twist of his cheeks showing anger, confusion.

Hanley's eyes was like holes in a blanket. He come lashing forward. 'By Gawd—'

166

'Shut up,' Cantress said, very cold, very clearly. 'I'm getting damn tired with your butting in every time I give one of the boys an order. Pack your junk, Andrade, and hit the trail.'

A shadow crossed Andrade's face like doubt. 'Hit the trail . . .' he echoed. 'Say—what the hell's bitin' you?'

Cantress said: 'You going, or ain't you?'

Andrade, plainly, was not up to getting it. He looked like he thought Ed Cantress was crazy.

Hanley must of guessed what Ed was up to. But he couldn't seem to think what he'd better do about it. I seen him open his mouth several times to speak, but he closed it each time without saying anything. The whole gang was watching him.

I could guess his trouble. He had built a shrewd trap for Cantress' catching; had seen Cantress in it. But the jaws hadn't closed and, being such a great trapper himself, he was worried now lest, someplace on this trail, somewhere well hidden in Cantress' words, there'd been a deadfall laid for himself to step into. He turned his intolerant stare on Andrade. 'You heard what the chief said, didn't you? Talk up then, damn you, an' give him a answer!'

In the brittle quiet, Bronc Andrade, caught again off guard, stood like a fool with his jaw dropped open. His baffled stare searched the

Texan sullenly. 'I don't see—'

What it was he didn't see wasn't to make no difference, because just then one of the other guys growled: 'What about this sneakin' tinbadge, Cantress? We goin' t' search—'

'I'm taking care of him,' Cantress said. 'Break it up now, boys. Get on back to your—'

Right then was when Andrade's mind quit working. He reached for his pistol.

Cantress' head came round with a gleam of teeth. Fireglow danced off the shine of metal. A white flame leaped from Cantress' hip.

Andrade's gun was still lifting when the lead smashed into him. He rocked on his heels with his mouth wide open, the pistol dropped from his wide-sprung fingers and the last shade of color rushed out of his cheeks. I saw him fall, all the swagger spilled out of him.

After Andrade's killing Cantress had ordered me tied. He seemed to have believed Hanley after all. He wasn't, anyways, taking any chances. He had fixed it so I couldn't run for it or make any trouble till they'd thrased out my fate, or whatever it was they'd gone off to do.

They'd left me tied by the campfire's embers but had taken no chances on my burning free. They'd tied my wrists firm and tight behind me, around the rough bole of a cottonwood tree. 'Just think things over,' Ed Cantress had told me. 'Maybe, time I come back, you'll have something to say.'

He hadn't posted no guards; but he didn't need any. Nothing would have pleased that bunch more than the chance to blow a few windows through me.

Then, sudden like, startled, I picked my ears up.

There was someone moving in. Through the brush. Real cautious.

Someone with a knife, I made no doubt.

Then I thought of Charlie. Good old Charlie, I thought, coming up to loose me.

But it wasn't Charlie.

It was Four-Eyes.

Tulare!

I felt him working on the ropes that were holding me.

I couldn't see him because he kept where the shadows was thickest, behind me. But I knew it was him when he whispered: 'Tonight—*right now*. You still feel up to it?'

'I might's well be shot for killin' Cantress, as shot for nothing,' I muttered bitterly. 'What'm I supposed to use for a hogleg?'

'This,' he said when the ropes fell free, and pressed a sixshooter into my fingers.

After that I didn't hear him no more.

Quite a while went by before I got enough feeling in my hands to move them. Then I felt for the gun; took a good long look at it.

A bad luck gun.

It was one of Andrade's. I could tell by the glow of its mother-of-pearl handles. But it was loaded all right.

I was getting up, slipping it into my half-breed holster, when close and soft I hear someone humming:

Oh, bury me not
On the lone prai-rie,
Where the coyotes howl
And the winds blows free—

'They'll be buryin' us,' I said, 'If we don't git out of here.'

Charlie chuckled. 'What was that four-eyed varmint up to? Turnin' you loose so the gang could gulch you?'

'Come to give me a gun,' I said. 'It's in his mind I'm goin' to kill Cantress.'

'Humph,' Charlie grunted. 'The's a lot in his mind besides his prayers. Here's somethin' for you I picked up in town.'

I looked at the letter he put in my hands. By leaning close I could see my name on it. *Ike Stroud, Esq. Care of Postmaster. Perry, Oklahoma.*

I didn't offer no jaw wagging. I opened the envelope and pulled out the paper. There was just one sheet. I looked at the signature. *Frank Wattrons.*

I guess my hand got to shaking. Took me quite a spell to make out his writing. There wasn't much of it. Characteristically brief, all the Judge said was: 'Nell worse. Doc says she's

170

got to go east for operation. Can you put up the money?'

I didn't know if I could or not. But I knew right off I would damn well try. Nell and me thought a heap of each other. There had always been strong ties between us. I expect our thoughts of each other was considerably colored by that need for affection that marks every orphan; I know—but no matter.

Charlie said, impatient: 'You goin' t' dream all night? If we're goin' t' pull out we better git started.'

No doubt about that. But the best chance I had to get that money was to rate promotion by busting this gang up. I couldn't expect the Judge to kick in for me—he'd done more than enough for the Strouds already.

I said: 'There's one or two things I got to tend to first. Meantime, you can be sneaking some broncs off an' pilin' the gear on. And I want back that knife you been packin' around for me. D'you know if O'Daye's still hangin' round camp?'

He said he didn't. Kind of reluctant-like he fetched out the knife there'd been so much talk about. Stood running his fingers over its handle. 'Look—' he said abruptly, earnestly. 'Let's heave this sorry damn thing in the brush. No good'll come of it—mark my word—'

'There's nothin' wrong with that knife,' I told him. 'It's all in the minds of the damn fools after it. Ed told the truth; that lizard

171

handle's plumb solid silver. There ain't no secret hollows or springs in it—'

'Jest the same,' he said, 'I wish you'd git rid of it. Where the's smoke the's fire. That knife's bad medicine—'

'So,' I grinned, putting the knife away, 'is this here pistol Tulare give me. But you won't catch me heavin' it off in the brush. Nor this pig-sticker, neither.'

I give him a good-natured slap on the shoulder. 'You go pile the hulls on a couple of fast ones an' lead 'em around to the back of Ed's cabin.'

I moved off, not giving him time to argue. But I couldn't help wondering as I strode through the dark who it was had stolen it from Ed in the first place. Tulare had give it to me that night him and Corva had caught me at Hanley's. But that didn't signify Tulare had stolen it. Might as well have been Corva—or Hanley, even.

But it didn't much matter, I thought, who had stole it. I'd things more important than that to worry with. Like, for instance, which it was Cantress figured me—Sundance or a marshal. Or did he think me both? And who was Sundance? Was it really Hanley? Or was it somebody else? Tulare, maybe?

It might even be Cantress.

I growled an oath and hastened my pace up. For all I could tell it might be old man O'Daye. A bitter taste come into my mouth when I thought of that dratted girl again. It made my guts ache to think how she'd diddled me. From first to last she'd loaded me handsome; made me look like a proper fool! And all the time me thinking her innocent—soft and sweet like a prairie rose!

She wasn't no better than Little Breeches Rose of the Cimarron or Cattle Annie!

I guessed Sundance was the whiskered Texan; it was him, all right, Bet had set her cap for. She had taken my note and give it to him—which reminded me I'd better be seeing Bill pronto. Bill Tilghman, I mean. If Doolin's crowd was heading north they was probably on their way to sack Ignalls. Ignalls was north—just beyond the border.

I opened the door of Cantress' shack.

Three men looked up—looked again, and stiffened.

Cantress, O'Daye and the whiskered Texan.

They'd been laying plans around a half killed bottle.

Even then I didn't get onto it rightly, didn't see Hanley's hand fixed so slick behind this. I'd a score to settle with that lying Texan, but first I'd got to fix things up with Cantress; got to show him if I could I was the only one for him.

It was strong in my mind that that knife would prove it.

I saw Hanley's grip clamp white on the table edge.

If I could just win Cantress back for a little

bit I could fix that Texan and get to hell out of here. I seen him watching me with a cold amusement, but even then I didn't tumble.

'Here,' I said, plenty loud and clear, 'is that damn blade you been pawin' the sod for.' And I slapped it down on the table in front of him, drove it deep in the wood with its handle up, quivering.

It buzzed like a snake, made a shine in the lamp glow.

Not till then did I glimpse the fine trap I'd walked into. It was the Texan's grin that showed me the jaws of it.

Too late I remembered Tulare's sly grin, the quick, oily smirks of that Mexican, Corva; the thousand and one little hints I'd not heeded . . . that brush-muted talk between Whiskers and Cantress when that damned old buck had done his prognosticating.

They had honed it up proper and I'd cut my own throat with it.

'Find the knife,' Hanley'd told him, 'an' you'll have the rascal!'

CHAPTER TWENTY-THREE

We was riding on our way, quirt-and-spurring for Perry, riding hellity larrup by the shortest cuts that looked like to get us to Perry and Tilghman. But we was traveling, mostly, for the good of our hides—and I take no shame, by God, for admitting it. Ed Cantress' bunch was strung out behind. Not far behind, neither. They wasn't picking no daisies. We didn't have to guess why they was riding their broncs down trying to come up with us.

Like I was still in the howling, frenzied thick of it, I could taste the wild peril I'd unloosed in that cabin; the stink of its powder, the stench of hot coal oil, the cries and the groans and the crash of its gun sound as flame wreathed muzzles drove lead through the murk on a search for soft bodies that were constantly shifted.

It was like a scene fresh torn out of hell.

Directly I'd realized the trap I'd stepped into I reached for my sixgun. My grip hadn't touched it when Hanley's arm come out like a sickle and batted the lamp clean across the room.

I got in first shot but I never hit nothing; I'd let go at Hanley, seen his whiskered mug ducking. After that the damned shack was a flame-streaked inferno.

I got out the door. I don't know how, but I done it. I felt the night air flowing cold crost my cheekbones. I could hear the scared shouts of the shot-wakened outlaws—the clatter of boots as they ripped through the bushes.

I run full tilt into a guy running towards me.

He grabbed for my arm as I was rushing my gun up. 'Save some o' yo' lead f' them others!'

Charlie's voice growls; then he was dragging me, pulling me hard round the cabin.

I seen the dark shapes of a pair of tall horses. They was pretty excited. We didn't waste no time getting onto them, neither.

'Which way?' Charlie yells.

'Town!' I said; and we was off like a cyclone.

We hit the creek, splashing the water of it every whichway. We tore off down the gulch like new hands with the mail.

'Hadn't we ort t' antigodle some—fuss up our sign a mite? It'll slow 'em down some—'

'Not them!' I said. 'They know damn well what place we'll be headin' for. Hanley knows I'm a tinbadge—they'll romp straight for Tilghman's.'

'All the mo' reason f' us not goin' there—'

I said, 'You let me take care of our directions, Charlie. I got business with Tilghman—plenty! I ought to've got hold of him five days ago.'

He didn't say nothing after that for awhile. I reckon he was doing some powerful tall thinking. Probably, I thought, he was trying to see where traveling with me was like to land him.

'Don't worry about my star,' I told him. 'I ain't forgettin' all the help you gave me. If things work out right, I'll get you a guard's job with me.'

He didn't say much; didn't commit himself one way or the other. But I could tell he was thinking.

'Wait a second,' he said, and slid out of the saddle. I seen him squat; whip the scarf off his neck, spread it flat on the ground and put his ear against it. An old Injun trick for hearing hoofbeats.

When he finally lifted his check from the earth, retrieved his scarf and got up again, though his tone was hearty I caught puzzlement in it. 'By grab, Ike,' he said, getting into his saddle, 'we've shook 'em.'

'Maybe,' I said, dubiously eyeing the grass flats stretching away to the east and west of us, 'there's some other way round. It's a cinch they've guessed what I'm headed for. Maybe they've short-cut us some way—'

'I ain't never heard of no sho't cuts.'

'But that don't prove there ain't none.'

'What the hell could they do if they *did* beat us in?'

'Plenty,' I said. 'They could ride into town an' murder Bill Tilghman, catchin' him unawares an' all. They could cache themselves out in some of them buildin's an' pick us off soon's we showed on the street. Or,' I said grimly, 'they might do both.'

'Ahr,' Charlie scoffed, 'You're workin' up nightmares. Ain't no sho'ter way than this.'

'Well,' I said, 'I'm hopin' you're right.'

*　　　*　　　*

177

Day was coloring sky's gray shading time we finally sighted Perry. There was scores of lights from oil lamps and lanterns, with flares and cook fires quartered around them thicker than flies round a sorghum barrel. An all-night stand, mighty proud and blatant, the streets fair writhing with jammed humanity. Made my fears, of a sudden, look mighty foolish; didn't seem like anyone'd tackle nothing *this* big.

Just the same, Doolin had. His wild bunch had come in and raided the Buckhorn—right in daylight, if you could believe the stories. I made up my mind to proceed with caution. I wouldn't be helping *no* one, dead.

There was a hective stream of life clogged its streets. Boomers, new settlers, hands from the ranges, soldiers, traders and the riffraff that ever dogs all land booms was scurrying back and forth like pack rats. You could hear all kinds of talk and rumors. Owlhooters' names was the most repeated. Tall, spiked heels and clank of spurs made a steady rumble of sound like a war drum, swelled and bolstered by the clack of jaw wagging. Here some fellow yelled to a neighbor; there some bullwhacker made his whip pop. Color and noise was the two biggest things in the town of Perry—unless you was taking a count of the tinhorns.

We wasn't the only guys riding, by any means. Wagons and horses was cluttered so thick it was all you could do to force a way

178

through them, and most of the time the chin of my bronc was being rode free on the nag's rump ahead.

'Gawd's gullet!' breathed Charlie, sleeving off his wet face, 'I'll take jail any day to crawlin' through this!'

From a road cutting into our lane from the left a sheriff's posse come shouting and cursing, swinging their quirts to lash a way past us. I seen their quarry, a blue shirted breed with a band round his hair, wipe the blood off his knife on a cavalryman's coat tail, thumb his nose at the posse and tramp off up an alley.

Charlie snorted. 'How's yo' head?' he said; and I was amazed to find I had plumb forgot the pains I'd been nursing not so many hours back.

We had finally pried ourselves from the traffic, was paused in an oasis by a crowded hitchrack.

'C'mon,' I said, swinging out of the saddle. 'We'll make better time shanksmarin' it now. Be a lot less like to get shot in the back, too. Bill's office's just around this corner.'

We left our broncs and got onto the walk, took the jolting and jostling with the rest of the herd. One beetle-browed sodbuster tromped plumb on my corns, but I never did nothing more than give him a look. He muttered something and was gone behind us.

We was rounding the corner when Charlie, sudden like, reached out a hand like a vise and

179

stopped me.

I seen right off what the kid was scowling at. Yonder was the shack that housed Bill's office. There was a big crowd around it.

'What's up?' I asked a frock-coated gambler.

Fellow shook his head, give a kind of dry whistle. He dragged a deep breath into him that must of gone, by the sound, clean down to his boot heels. 'Gent just got killed in there— one of Bill's deputies. He's in there now with blood all over him. Bunch of horsemen come up and emptied their guns at the place. Buck had the bad luck to be inside it.'

I looked at Charlie. Charlie looked at me.

'Where's Tilghman?'

'Nobody knows,' the gambler answered. 'Left town, I heard, yesterday evening. They might know over at the livery stable—'

'My Gawd!' Charlie gasped, quick's we'd rounded the corner. 'You was right—right as rain!'

'We better go eat—'

Charlie just looked at me. 'You kin go eat if you want to—'

'All right,' I said. 'We'll go hunt that stable.'

But the boss, when we found it, hadn't no idea where Bill had went to. ' 'Course,' he said, 'it might be he's gone after Doolin. Still, it don't noways seem likely. News never got here till after—'

'News?—what news?'

'Doolin's raid on Cimarron. Ain't you heard? From all accounts he musta sacked the place, broke 'er plumb wide open an' left 'er in ashes. Them Kansas law-packers—'

I never waited to hear no more of it.

We was back on the main drag, headed for the horses, before Charlie caught up enough wind to put questions. 'This ain't no time for talkin',' I told him. 'Ingalls ain't more'n a two hours' ride from Cimarron. Ain't a chance we can get there in time to do anything, but I'm goin' to try.'

'You plumb crazy?'

'Deal to be said for it,' I told him, bitter. ' 'Bout the only thing I can qualify for.'

'But Cimarron.' Charlie wailed despairingly, 'is damn neah two hundred mile f'om heah! What sense is there takin' a pasear like that t' stop a play that'll be over an' done with 'fore we can much as ever git started?'

'I've *got* to—can't you see that, Charlie? We knew they was figurin' a raid on Ingalls. I should of gotten that dope—'

'You *tried*. Ain't yo' fault if that note—'

'Color don't count if the colt won't trot. Good intentions never hanged no owlhooters, Charlie. I've botched this job from the time I started. If I can grab some luck I've a chance to square myself—'

'A damn slim chance, 'f you're figgerin' to beat Bill Doolin to Ingalls!'

I knew it. Hardly a chance in a million. But I

had to try.

'The's no use arguin'. I'm goin',' I said. 'You can do what you feel like; but long as there's a chance I can save a few lives or some honest man's property—'

'All right,' Charlie said disgusted. 'No need you singin' the chorus ag'in. If you're bound to go, I'll trail along with you.'

I walked a few steps trying to think what was best. I felt a deep surge of gratitude toward him. He was a likeable kid and his decision backed up what I'd felt all along, that despite his wild ways he was sound at heart. All he needed was guidance and he'd shape up fine.

But there wasn't much use in both of us going.

'You better stick here an' watch Cantress,' I said. 'He's—'

'I ain't Cantress' keeper!' Charlie bridled. ' 'Course,' he said with a shrug, 'if you don't want me along . . .'

'It ain't that I don't want you—'

'Good!' he grinned. 'When we leavin'?'

*   *   *

We made good time. It was a considerable journey, by horse, from Perry to Ingalls. I was wearing my deputy marshal's badge and we changed broncs frequent. Our roughest luck was in quitting Perry.

Charlie had run out of smoking. 'You go

fetch our nags,' he told me, 'while I run over to O'Daye's an' git some.'

'You watch out,' I said. 'O'Daye may be back, an' if he is you're like to have trouble. If you see him in there, you better go someplace else for your smokin'.'

Charlie just grinned and shoved his way through the crowd like old man O'Daye was the least of his troubles. I was of half a mind to go with him, on the chance I might see Betsy. But the things she had done . . . I tell you, it made me mad every time I thought of her. Cuddling up to me the way she had, leading me on, getting me so I couldn't tell up from down, and her all the time hitched snug to Cantress! I said, 'To hell with her!' and let him go. He was old enough to look out for himself if he was ever going to be able to, I reckoned.

I wasn't twenty yards from where I'd left our horses when I heard the rattle of gunfire break out from the direction of old man O'Daye's, and I cussed myself for letting Charlie go over there.

I didn't rightly know what to do. It was dollars to doughnuts he'd run smack into some of Cantress' bunch, and if he had he'd be needing all the help he could get. But right now was when he was needing it. Time I got there it would probably be over, and I hadn't no business to be mixing in it noway; my job was to ride word to Ingalls.

While I stood there, hesitating, the firing

183

quit.

I seen a couple guys staring the same way I was. But, mostly, the crowd wasn't paying no mind to it. Shootings, I guessed, was the commonest thing they had in this neighborhood.

I made up my mind. I said to hell with Ingalls. Charlie was too fine a kid to be left in the lurch with a bunch of damn wolves like the Cantress outfit.

I was shoving forward, not much caring what the shoved ones thought of it just so they got themselves out of my way, when 'Hey—*Ike!*' someone sings out behind me, and there was Charlie with a wide grin on him. 'Over there ain't wheah we left them broncs.'

I said: 'I know it ain't. I was comin' over to knock some sense in you.' It kind of made me mad, seeing him so cheerful after all my worrying. 'What was the shootin'?'

'Some down-an'-out boomer reckoned t' rob O'Daye's store.'

'Get him?'

'Naw—never even seen 'im,' Charlie said. 'When I heard the shootin' I went someplace else—'

A loud commotion busted out behind us. A raw-boned, hatless, red shirted farmer, with his eyes rolling wild-like, was plowing through the crowd like a Kansas twister. There was two-three others coming right along behind him. The red shirted gent yelled: 'There he is!

184

That's the feller! That—'

'C'mon!' Charlie grunted, and broke into a run. He waved his arms like the fellow behind us. 'Stop 'im!' he clamored. 'Stop that owlhoot!—that black-hatted jasper!'

He cut aslant my path, dragging me with him toward the nearest hitchrack. 'Grab a hawse,' he muttered, 'an' let's git outta here.'

A gun started blasting the bedlam back of us. Shots whined past us and the crowd begun scattering. A slug nicked my hat and I took his advice. I ducked under the tierail and snatched a bronc's reins loose.

The uproar behind us had grown like Jack's beanstalk. Half the guns in Perry seemed to be adding their voice to the frantic racket. Splinters and dust was jumping up everyplace; there didn't seem to be much choice as to targets. The whole rack of horses was raring and snorting when the back of my lap hit the deck of a saddle.

It was then that I discovered that the hull I was forking hadn't no least relation to the reins I was clutching.

I let them go like they was hot potatoes.

There wasn't no chance to make a swap in saddles. There wasn't no chance to do nothing, seemed like. The reins of the bronc I had got astride of was still calm-wrapped round the swell of the tierail. Lead was smacking all around me like hailstones, and it begun to seep through me this wasn't no mistake.

There was only one thing to do, and I done it. I grabbed the horn and clapped in the spurs. The bronc lunged forward like a case of dynamite. The tierail snapped. The reins snapped, too. The next few seconds was a impossible blur of scared faces and buildings rocketing past with the speed of a cyclone.

And then we was clear, taking out between tents on a dash for the prairie.

I reached and got hold of the dangling rein ends; they was almighty short but they'd do, I guessed, till I could rig something better. I seen Charlie ahead of us and spurred the nag towards him.

CHAPTER TWENTY-FOUR

Ingalls, when we got there, was a-buzz with talk of Doolin. It was not a big place but it was plenty excited. Despite current rumors rocking Perry, Cimarron, it seemed, had not been sacked. He had held up a Sante Fe train just outside it and had dug for the tules in considerable hurry with a posse of marshals hot on his trail. They had, we learned, chased him south into Oklahoma. He'd been wounded, so the story went, and was believed holed up in a ranch down there. 'But he'll be back,' they said, 'and when he comes we'll plant him!'

I seen Charlie's lip curl up at their confidence; but a few minutes later I was inclined to agree with them. I heard my name called and turned to see Jim Masterson— brother to the famous 'Bat'—step out of the hotel and come striding towards us. He shook my hand warmly. 'Bill,' he said, 'passed on your message. There's quite a bunch of us. All we're waitin' for now is Doolin.'

I stared. 'Mind ridin' that trail again?' I said.

He give me a searching look and said, 'Bill passed on the word of what Doolin's planning—his plans to raid Ingalls. We're all set here to give him a hot reception. Got the pick of the Fort Smith marshals hid here. John Hixon, me, Lafe Shadley, Dick Speed an' Houston. Bill's comin', too.'

'Bill Tilghman?'

'Who else?' Jim grinned. 'Doolin won't get away from us this time.'

I was pretty much tangled up in my mind, wondering how Bill had got the word to them when I hadn't even managed to get it to him. I reckoned someone else must of tipped Doolin's hand to him.

I introduced Charlie. 'He's workin' with me,' I said. 'Make a pretty fair hand when he's growed a little. Where you all holed out—here in town?'

Masterson shook his head. 'Nope. All out in the brush. Idea is to let the wild bunch ride in to town, then we'll close in on 'em and bag the whole outfit. Be a damn nice haul—law's posted five thousand on Doolin alone. You fellows better ride out and see Late Shadley. He'll post you an' give you your places.'

I knew these marshals who had come to bag Doolin. They weren't crusaders or bible tract salesmen; they weren't over-worried about rules of law and order. They was fighting men, plain ordinary humans who wasn't about mixing an occasional feud with their justice. They was men of prowess, iron-nerved, proud of their skill.

Lafe Shadley's welcome was quiet to brusqueness. He didn't shake hands nor waste no words. 'Tilghman won't be with us,' he said. 'Team run away an' he got his leg broke. Doolin's ridin' in now. We won't have to wait long.'

'Where you want us?'

'Right here,' Shadley said. 'You'll stick with me.'

We climbed off our horses and hunkered down to wait.

There was a lot of queer notions ramming round through my head. I couldn't seem to get it straight how Tilghman had managed to get this crew gathered. Nor was I having much luck keeping my thoughts off Betsy, though I'd told myself more than forty-'leven times a growed man wouldn't waste his time with loose women—leastways, not no man that had any pride. And there was that shooting I'd heard back at Perry to bother me, not to mention how come all them shots was flung at us.

Charlie's set forth his notions while I was tying up the reins with some pieces of rope. 'Funny,' he said, 'about all that shootin'.'

'Yeah. Very,' I says, keeping on with my labors. 'Quite a passle of it, wasn't there?' I'd had my own ideas about what had caused it. But when I looked at his face I changed my mind.

He give me a kind of odd, startled look. Then he drew back his head and laughed till the tears come. 'Oh, gar!' he says, rubbing his eyes out. 'You didn't think 'twas *me* they was shootin' at, did you? By grab! I b'lieve you been thinkin' I tried t' rob O'Daye's store!' There was a regretful glint in the way his eyes twinkled. 'Wished I'd thought of it,' he muttered.

A rider eased out of the trees and had a talk with Shadley. Shadley took a look round. 'Doolin's here,' he said. 'They've just come in. This is going to be easy. They ain't in good shape to put up much fight. Doolin's still havin' trouble with his foot, an' Arkansaw Tom's so bad hurt they've put him to bed in a secon' floor room at the hotel. Reckon they're aimin' to rest up before they start anything. Just as well. Give us a chance to bag 'em before any damage's done.

'Now here's the lay,' he told us, quiet like. 'Our posse's busted into little groups that'll all be closing in on Mister Doolin's boys together. No shootin', mind you, till I give the word— unless, of course, they try to break for the open. If they do, just remember they're wolves. We'll move in now.'

Easing through the timber I was glad there was going to be a stop put to Doolin; but it didn't please me none to think what Cantress might be doing while all the law was here stretching their loop to corral the wild bunch. We was leaving Perry fair prey to his outfit, and he wasn't the kind to be overlooking it, neither. Him and Sundance . . . Made me feel a heap bitter when I thought of Sundance. I'd been sent in here to make an end of Sundance.

We left our horses before we quit the brush. We took up positions back of a barn and a hay shed. From where we was we could see several others of the posse spread out to either side of us, taking cover behind the fences and wagons. Lafe Shadley said, 'Stroud—suppose you go in and tell Doolin he's surrounded. Give him a chance to give up, if he wants to.'

I nodded. Climbed over a fence and walked towards the hotel. I wasn't feeling too happy. I wasn't scared of Bill Doolin. But some of his gang I wouldn't trust with a pea shooter.

I didn't have very far to walk. Ingalls wasn't much more than a bump in the road. A hotel, a saloon, two or three stores and a livery stable, and about a dozen houses. I seen right off where the gang had left their horses; they was all at the livery barn. I seen Bitter Crick George loafing round with the stableman.

I felt my hair rise when he turned around, looked across the road at me. I seen him pull up his brows, seen his shoulders stiffen. He muttered something at the stableman, sharp like.

I said: 'Howdy, George. Pretty good day you've picked to get buried on.'

I seen his goatee twitch; seen him beetle his brows up. Then he smiled, and it wasn't no grimace like you'd get from a thug. A plain smile, an amused one, though a pressure of months creased deep lines round his eyes and the cant of his shoulders come forward, swift lowering. A to-hell-with-the-cost sort of look it gave him with his neat little hands thumb-tucked in his gun belt. 'How are you, Ike? See you're wearin' your badge again. Kind of outa grounds, ain't you?'

'You did yourself no service, George, when you aired Bill's plans in the Buckhorn last week.'

No change touched his eyes. He rolled up a smoke, struck a light on his thumbnail. 'Bob done his best to get me broke of that.'

'It's a habit won't bother you after today. Go tell Bill Doolin—'

'Tell him what?' Doolin said.

And there he was, tall and lank as ever. Just stepped round the corner in his cat-footed way. There was a rifle couched in the crook of

191

his elbow. He looked just like folks said he did, with his tall slouch hat and sandy hair, with the long-shanked spurs a-clank on his boot heels.

'Tell him what?' he asked smoothly.

I was a damn good target, in the middle of the road, standing spang in the slant of the hot, gushing sunlight. Not that I was hot—there was goosebumps all over me. But a Fort Smith law packer don't back down.

I said, 'You better give up. Better give up peaceable. You ain't got a chance. We got you plumb surrounded.'

'That so?' Bill says. He never batted an eyelash. 'Whereabouts do you bury your dead, Mister Stroud?'

I said: 'This ain't no joke. If you want to stay safe—'

'Safe ain't never been a part of my lingo—'

'Bein' dead'll seem kind of strange to you, too. But you got your choice. Lafe Shadley says you can surrender or—'

'You tell Lafe Shadley he can go to hell!'

*   *   *

I told him.

'All right, boys,' Shadley said. 'Smoke 'em out.'

It appeared like the gang was pretty well scattered. Doolin and Newcomb had disappeared pronto. There wasn't no firing coming out of the stable, but some of them

192

buildings was spitting right copious. There was just one thing in the minds of that gang, a simon-pure craving to get to their horses. There wasn't none of them scared to try, neither. Every little while some damn fool would try it, dart into the street or duck off between buildings. There'd be a big burst of firing. You could see the dust jumping up all around him, and sometimes you'd see the dust jump from the clothes he wore. If he kept to his feet you'd see him scuttle for shelter.

But the firing wasn't one-sided by any means. There was a handy shot firing from one of the hotel's second floor windows—a damn good shot, and he'd plenty to pick from. He killed one fellow that wasn't three feet from me. 'Arkansaw Tom,' Lafe Shadley said.

He wasn't too sick to handle a rifle.

Marshal Houston said: 'Four-five of you boys turn your guns on that window.' We done it, and Tom got away from it almighty sudden.

It seems like we'd ought to of had them outlaws sewed up. But all over town they was creeping and crawling, and the hell of it was they was making good headway. There was some of them now pretty close to the stable.

All of a sudden I heard a grunt back of me. I looked around quick and I seen Houston falling. He was all doubled up. There was blood pouring out of him. Charlie pointed toward the hotel roof just as another of the posse pitched forward. I seen a rifle barrel glinting where it stuck from the shingles. 'It's that damn Arkansaw Tom!' Shadley gritted.

'If one of us,' Charlie said, 'c'ld make out t' sneak over there, he c'ld set the damn shack afire—that'd fix him.'

'Smart idea,' Shadley said. 'Go ahead.'

I wasn't too crazy to try such foolishness. But if Charlie was game to I'd be damned if I wasn't. So we started over, creeping cautious.

We was halfway there when Charlie sings out: 'Theah's thet Bitter Crick jasper—see 'im? To the left. By the corner of thet buildin'.'

It was George, all right. He seen us, too. He flung up his rifle. Charlie's first shot smashed it. Newcomb dropped the wrecked rifle and grabbed out his six guns. I could feel his lead smacking hard all around me. 'Run!' I yelled, jumping up; and took a final shot at him. I seen him stagger. Then we was round the corner and lost to sight of him.

I found out later that his girl was in town. 'Rose of the Cimarron' was what they called her. She was in the hotel—had seen the whole business. She knew he was wounded; guessed his guns empty. She run to his room, which was on the second floor right next to Arkansaw's, grabbed his extra gun and a belt of fresh shells, ripped a sheet off the bed and lowered them out a window that didn't look on the battle. She tied a couple more sheets together and let herself after them. We seen her a couple seconds later when she ran across the road in the thick of the shooting to give them to Bitter Crick.

We had all we could do though without trying to stop her. Mrs. Pierce, the landlady, seen us outside the back door. She guessed right away what we had in mind. She said if we wouldn't set fire to her place, she'd go up and make Tom come down and surrender.

We said all right; we'd give her two minutes.

Couple seconds later a rifle and two empty pistols come banging down. The rifle damn near brained old Charlie—would have, I mean, if it ever had hit him. It didn't miss him more than two or three whiskers. While he was cussing, Mrs. Pierce led Arky out. He sure was a mess. He was bleeding all over. But he wasn't wound up by a long shot, yet. He made a wild grab, just missing my hardware.

'Listen—' I said. 'I don't know you from Adam—no skin off my nose what happens to you. Dead freight packs a heap better'n the kickin' kind. Just an idea to cling to if you want to keep healthy.'

He, give me a roll of his bloodshot eyes. He wasn't a half bad looking kind of jasper. Long sort of face with a big, sweeping mustache. There was a big welt across it. There was blood in his mustache. 'I won't give you no trouble,' he finally said, meek-like.

'Glad to hear it,' I told him, and said to Charlie: 'Keep your eye skinned.'

I slid along the wall till I come to the corner.

I took a quick look round it, trying to gauge if I could the extent of the battle; what progress, if any, the marshals might be making. All the firing now seemed to be centered round the livery stable. There wasn't any great pile of it. Just a few random poppings.

I rejoined Charlie. Told him about it. Arkansaw nodded. 'They're all in the stable. Me an' Bitter Crick,' he said, 'is the only ones couldn't make it.'

I tramped through the hotel but the place was empty. Everybody'd hopped it—even the landlady. I went back and asked Arkansaw where George Newcomb was. Before he could answer Charlie turned me around so I faced the street. Wasn't no reason for nobody saying nothing.

Bitter Creek was out there with Rose of the Cimarron. She had both arms clapped round him and was half carrying, half dragging him in the direction of the stable. I eyed them hard and I felt like smashing something.

The posse kind of waited till she got him inside. Then every gun in the crowd cut loose. Lead drummed the walls like a rattle of hailstones. That stable must of damn near been riddled with bullets. Doolin's gang, trapped there, couldn't of lived twenty minutes and Doolin must of known it. In a lull in the firing you could hear them arguing.

Then I hear Dick Speed's voice raised in a bellow. 'There they go!' he shouted, jumping into plain sight. 'Out the back!' he cried, and flung up his rifle.

But they hadn't all run for it. Two had stayed to cover them. Bill Dalton and Doolin. Doolin stepped out of the barn cold as frog legs. He shot from the hip.

Dalton said: 'Bill—you missed him.'

Doolin, with the whole damn push of us throwing lead at him, got down on one knee and rested his elbow. When he fired again Speed threw up his arms. His rifle fell out of them. He bent, sort of groped for it; fell on top of it.

'You got him that time,' Dalton called.

I caught a quick glimpse of Bitter Creek, out back, staggering and cursing, trying to get on his horse. I must of got him a lot worse than I guessed. Looked like he wasn't going to make it even with Rose bolstering him.

I heard Doolin call to him. Wished the damn fool would get down or behind something. But he didn't. Just stood there, peering at Newcomb. 'You goin' to make it?' he called.

'Sure,' answered George. 'I'll git there someway. Don't mind about me.'

Rose got up on the horse in front of him. He swayed against her, wrapping both arms round her. There was a lot of lead flying. I don't know how much of it was directed at them. Last I seen of them they was both still riding.

When I looked back the two Bills was mounted; Doolin and Dalton. We triggered like hell but they got away from us.

'They can't git far!' Shadley gritted. 'My Gawd—we most nigh cut 'em to pieces!'

We run for our horses. Got them and followed.

After a while we seen Rose and George. They had fell behind; they was off the horse now. We seen the horse loping off to the left. The girl was trying to drag Bitter Creek into the turkey brush. She was game all right, game clean to her toenails.

'There comes Doolin an' Dalton!' somebody cried.

'Good!' Shadley said. 'We'll bag all three of 'em!'

Some of the deputies with us wasn't looking too high round the gills, I noticed. I didn't much blame them. Bitter Creek George, when it come to a shootout, wasn't no guy to turn up your nose at—not even if he was dying, which I didn't think he was. And his girl could handle a gun like a trooper; she was near as well known as Calamity Jane. Or Belle Starr, far as that went. Bill Dalton, neither, wasn't no one to sneer at. Though he hadn't ever ridden with his train-robbing brothers, it wasn't for any lack of wanting to on his part. Emmett Dalton has claimed they plain wouldn't let him. He had a wife and two children and they wanted him to go straight, but it just wasn't in him.

Doolin and Dalton, jumping from their horses, ducked into the brush with their six-shooters blazing. Jim Masterson, just beside me, swore. I emptied my gun, firing fast, at Doolin. I don't think even one of my shots nicked him. Three answering shots jerked my hat simultaneous. I dropped, hastily fumbling fresh loads from my shell belt. I heard a wild yell from Sheriff John Hixon. I see Dalton's horse go end over end. We done our best to smoke them boys out of there.

They had more guts than you could hang on a fencepost.

Somebody—Masterson, I think—scored a hit on Dalton. I seen him jump straight out of the brush. He tripped and pitched into a ditch and lay there. I could see his right arm, useless, doubled up under him.

Then Hixon's son let out a squawk. Above the banging of pistols I could hear hoofs pounding. I whirled; stared yonder. Help was coming. But not for us. Some of the wild bunch, come back to help Doolin. I seen the mugs of the first couple plain; fellow called Buck and Little Dick. They started shooting quick as they seen us.

Doolin never even turned to look around. Broad-shouldered and hatless, he was crouched above Bitter Creek with both guns smoking. Odds hadn't never bothered *him* none—he'd of taken on a army if it got in his way. You couldn't hardly help admiring him, kind of. He had more guts than a fiddle band.

His left hand gun gouted flame again. Lafe Shadley jerked forward, fell out of his saddle.

The posse was routed. Both sides of me broncs were wheeling, racketing off under that withering fire. I kept thumbing my hammer but nothing happened. Doolin still crouched there, firing, eyes glinting; colder than hell on the stoker's day off. I see him drop his gun, jump forward and wrench Lafe Shadley's from the marshal's dead fingers, I chopped at his head with my gun barrel—missed him. Heard the grunt of his breath as he straightened, gun lifting.

That was when I let my horse have his way.

CHAPTER TWENTY-FIVE

Well, we was just one more of the countless posses that had busted its horns trying to gore Bill Doolin. Doolin had give us the horse laugh proper. Our grand attempt, the fine, tall ambush I'd set such store by, had cost us the lives of three first class marshals. We had Arkansaw Tom to show we'd jumped Doolin, but Bill and the rest of his wild bunch had vanished.

I was done. I knew it. I had failed completely. Thought of Nell was in my mind like a knifeblade. Instead of the promotion I'd taken so much risk for I'd be lucking if they didn't set me guarding a wagon. Everything I'd touched had gone plumb haywire. I knew no more about Sundance now than I had when Yoe had first give me my orders—I hadn't even give any help to Bill Tilghman. The owlhooter breed had fair thrived on my strivings. If Fort Smith wouldn't own me I'd probably hang for a horse thief.

Defeat was bitter as gall in my mouth. How I'd get Nell east was beyond my figuring.

Night dragged along a brief message from Tilghman; a man fetched it over from the telegraph at Cimarron. Seemed like Bill was at Perry with his leg in a splint. I was to report to him pronto.

Been in touch with Fort Smith, like as not, I thought. Yoe's prob'ly told told him to pick up my badge. I went over to the saloon. 'Time to ride,' I told Charlie.

*   *   *

I'd as soon of had a corpse for a saddle pard as him, that night. He seemed to be in one of his mouth-harping moods and played all the lost chords the hills had ever listened at.

I told him, 'For Gawd's sake quit that cater-waulin'!'

We rode, after that, in a unrelieved silence.

About nine the third night we reached the outskirts of Perry.

201

The air was damp and smelled of wet grass, but it wasn't till a long time later I thought of it. At the moment I had things a heap more important for my mind to wrestle with: Like what I would do if Bill *was* going to fire me.

I didn't have much doubt but what Bill'd been told to fire me. Good intentions and excuses didn't count for much in the star packing business. Results was what Judge Parker looked at. The results I'd got wasn't nothing to be bragged on. I hadn't got Sundance. I hadn't busted up no gangs.

But three days' worth of thinking had showed me one thing. Sundance was connected someway with Ed Cantress; during the days I'd been with him every job the gang tackled had been jumped by Sundance. If it wasn't Hanley's hairy mug sneering at the law back of Sundance's flour sack, it sure as hell was Ed Cantress' or Tulare's. It *had* to be, damn it!

I had a forlorn notion to give it one more stab before I let Bill take my badge away. I say I had the notion. That's all it was. All the thinking my head was able to cope with was I'd got to get some money—a whole heap of it—quick like—if Nell was going to be sent east to a doctor.

We was passing a ramshackle barn when Charlie swung down and tossed me his reins. 'Hoof shaper lives heah I'm wantin' a word with. Wait a sec, will you?'

Charlie come back and got into his saddle. He sat awhile then, glumly twirling his ring. 'I got some news but it ain't very good. Sundance's been in an' robbed O'Daye's store. Ol' man was there an' Sundance killed him. Girl wasn't, though. Somethin' funny 'bout her—'

'You can leave her out of it,' I said real short. 'That all you learned?'

'Lot of tough gents hangin' round the Express Office, Joe says. Been siftin' in all evenin'—'

I said, 'It's time we was siftin' over to see Bill Tilghman.'

We was walking our broncs through a back alley's shadows, heading for the place where Bill was put up at, when Charlie bent sideways and reached for my bridle. 'Pull up!' he said urgent, sort of under his breath. 'Make out like we're arguin'. Quick's you can do it casual, look left.'

I said, 'All I see is the back of that bank—'

'More left. Take a squint in them cottonwoods,' Charlie said. 'See them hawses? Now look straight acrost. At the back of that feed store.'

There was no mistaking that shape in the shadows.

It belonged to Ed Cantress.

Nor was he alone. Farther down, near the back of the stage company's office, a second loitering figure showed briefly and faded.

Deep in the gloom of the yonder cottonwoods my stare picked up the glow of a cigarette. Remembrance of something—something Bet had said, laid icy fingers across my spine. That plan!—that wildcat trick for trapping Cantress with a tale of bullion in the stage company's office.

Because I had not killed Ed Cantress for her she'd taken it into her own hands now. Infatuated with the whiskered Hanley she was taking this means to free herself for him, never stopping to learn before she'd started that Tilghman was helpless with a busted leg, that the town was completely drained of lawmen. I saw no cause to rejoice in her ruse. By the way Cantress' men was strung out yonder I could guess pretty well what the man was up to. Doolin had come here and cleaned out the Buckhorn; Sundance had come and cleaned out O'Daye. Cantress' vanity must conjure something better, something brasher and more—much more, spectacular. He meant to gut the Express Office and top it off with the bank for good measure!

There was just one thing left to do, and I done it! I hauled Charlie into the dark between buildings. 'If you've an extra pistol,' I said, 'let me have it.' He dragged one out of his hip pocket. I took it. 'Go round up some men. An' get a move on,' I told him.

Leading his horse he started. Then stopped. 'Wheah'll I meet you?'

'In hell, like enough,' I said. 'Damn you—*git goin'!*'

*   *   *

I was putting his gun away there in the darkness, figuring to slip the thing into my shirt. But it hung up on something; or, leastways, I thought it did. I reached down, impatient, to see what was holding it. It was cloth, all right, but it wasn't my shirt. I got the thing free of the sight; put the gun away. Charlie's handkerchief probably, got snagged—It was then my fingers felt the holes that was in it.

I went still as stone, hardly breathing as the implications of this thing burst over me.

It was crazy—screwy as hell. But I had to make sure; had to know, for certain, one way or the other. I dropped the cloth. Struck a match in cupped palms and killed it instantly. But I couldn't shut out what its flare had shown me.

Like it or not, there on the ground lay the last lean link of the proof I needed—the one thing it took to jog my mind and drop every last clue snug into place.

Small wonder I'd sensed a connection between Sundance and Cantress' outfit! A bitter pill for a man to acknowledge, but Charlie Kaintuck was the outlaw, Sundance.

There on the ground, between my knees,

was a flour sack hood with two eyeholes cut in it. All the proof any marshal would ever ask for. Charlie, of course, wouldn't call it that. I could hear him scoff—almost hear him chuckle. But we'd got past the place where a chuckle could save him. The edge was curled back from his ingenious ways now.

It was Charlie, all right. I could tell, deep inside me. I remembered the ring I had seen on Sundance, that square, turquoise ring, Injun mounted in silver. On his middle finger it had been when he brought that gun barrel down on my head. Charlie had that ring on right now. Tonight.

I recalled the wild times that we'd been through, and shared. I could see his face in a thousand guises, mostly laughing, always reckless. The remembered twinkle of his boy's bright eyes; his swaggering poses, his aping of outlaws. And back of it all he had been the greatest—the fool of a kid who had taken us all in.

The bandit . . . Sundance.

The main stem of my orders. The man whose death I'd been told to contrive.

He should of spelled, to me, just one thing—promotion; the needed increase in pay that would send Nell east. There was, too, on his scalp, a cool fifteen thousand. Enough, I thought, to hire a hundred specialists. Enough, anyway, to see Nell through.

It was then I heard it, that deep, muffled

whoom! and the racketing crash that was the bank's door falling . . . the waterfall tinkle of glass shards dropping.

I moved without thought. Slapped my horse snorting streetward. I grabbed Charlie's gun; grabbed Bronc Andrade's out, too. Like a man half asleep I walked into the alley.

There was no one in sight. Not even Ed Cantress. He was gone from his place against the wall of the feed store. But the horses were still being held in the cottonwoods. 'Fine!' I said grimly. 'They'll not leave without horses.'

I was halfway there when the horse guard saw me. The wind from his shot whipped a whine past my cheekbones. I kept walking. The man fired again, the flash of his muzzle light weird in the tree gloom. Frantic, now, the fellow emptied his pistol. He was whirling to run when I fired. Just once.

A choked quiet followed the sound of the pistols.

'Fifteen thousand,' I said to myself.

And then a man's wild yell slammed scared down the alley. *'The Cantress gang—they're lootin' the bank! Look out! Look out! It's the Cantr—'* A gun went off somewhere out front; the swift, sharp cracking of rifles immediately swelling that one burst of sound to a rataplan bedlam of tumultuous discord. A man came out of the Express Company's office. I fired, saw him reel—go lurching inside again. The black rectangle of the bank's open doorway showed a red bleach of flame—black figures against it, into which I fired, hearing some man's yell shear to desperate thinness. A barrel-toned voice came out of the Express Office: 'Rush him, you fools, 'fore the whole town gits here!'

It was like a spark in a keg of powder, fusing fear and desire into action. I could see them bunching in the bank's lit doorway, black, sullen shapes against the fire they had kindled. Flame-tongues leaped from their lifted pistols. I lifted the stock of Andrade's belt gun, drove lead from its barrel till the hammer clicked dully against exploded shells that had no more life in them. The rush was broken, stopped and scattered in the swirling shadows that hemmed the bright doorsill. Two sprawled shapes lay awash in the fire glow, and the bull-toned one's bellow nor ought else could stir them.

Distant yells bit into and through the echoes as men spilled out of saloons and brothels; the rush of their booted feet grew plainer; a burst of firing out front told its hard, thin story of time grown short to the desperate men bitter crouched in the shadows. I yanked loose the reins of half a dozen horses, sent them pelting away through the night.

I was jamming fresh loads in my emptied pistol when the bull-toned man loosed his shout again, his timbered voice snapping out like a whiplash, urging them, flailing them, frantic, contemptuous—it came to me, sudden, it was the voice of Cantress, and I marveled at the extent of the change there was in it. Borne in off the plains came a train's whooing whistle. One red eye of flame lanced from the Express Office, the slug biting past me so close I could taste it; then every shadow became a springboard for violence as Cantress' voice drove his men at the trees again. The night was filled with the leaping shapes of them, curdled and criss-crossed with the streaks of their gunfire. Hoof sound clattered across the uproar; a wild-yelling rider split the ranks of the outlaws—the pistol laced shadows were suddenly bounding with riders, and a shrieking voice lifted: 'Sundance! Sundance!'

The gun sound rose to a frenzied crescendo, fell away, fell away to a low, jerky, barking; and Charlie's voice said against my ear: 'My Gawd! Let's git outen this!'

I drove two shots at a man with a sack. Saw him stumble, pitch forward; saw the sack drop beside him. Saw a second shape rush, fold abruptly across it.

'C'mon!' Charlie muttered; began tugging my elbow.

My hammer banged on an empty cartridge. 'You can go if you want to . . . Sundance,' I said.

His fingers went stiff where they clamped round my elbow. The slog of his breath was the only sound out of him. Then a man burst

209

into the trees—a lumbering shape with an up-and-down gait that could belong to nobody else but that Texan.

I slid the hold-out gun from the strap of my holster; felt Charlie's fingers fall away from my arm. I said: 'Hanley—' and fired at his muzzle flash; watched him rock backwards, lurch sideways and buckle.

The battle sounds now had gone dim up the alley. Even as we listened the shots petered out, the uproar diminished, swift dissolving in voice sound. From the bank, too, the firelight was dimming perceptibly as the town's bucket handers brought it under control.

I watched Charlie's head come around in the darkness. 'So it *did* hang up on my peacemaker . . . I kinda thought it did, Ike. Well—' A faint regret seemed to ride through his voice; then he shrugged, shook his head. 'It's been a sorry damn—'

'Charlie,' I said, 'Don't never look back. Leave the past for mistakes. Most fellers' is full of 'em. It's the future that—'

'You mean . . .' The rest of his talk got hung up in his throat. He stared like he couldn't believe his own guessing. 'You mean,' he said, husky, 'you ain't takin' me in?'

'There's never a noose been built to hang you, kid.'

'But that raise you been workin' for! That—'

He came forward, lean hands locking hard to my shoulders. 'You can't do it, Ike—you jest

210

can't! Why, yore sister—'

What it was I don't know, but we whirled around, startled. There was a tall figure limned, bleak and black, in the bank glow, legs widely spraddled, its shape crouched and canted.

'Been a long trail, Sundance . . .'

My belly muscles knotted. A cold fear cramped them.

It was Cantress speaking. He had us covered like a blanket.

We hadn't a chance.

We took one anyhow.

Two reports belted upward and outward. Charlie's gun, unused, struck the ground, still loaded. Through a blur I saw his buckling shape follow it. They'll tell you I cried, but I never. It was that damn smoke from the bank in my eyes.

*   *   *

'You talk like an idjit!' Tilghman told me gruffly. 'You don't know *what* you'd have done—it's the facts that count, anyhow. The facts is plain an' they can't be twisted. Sundance's dead, ain't he?'

'But you don't understand—'

'All right then. They're both dead. Sundance and Cantress—you ain't denyin' you killed Cantress?'

'No.'

211

'All right then. You're in line for a raise. I'm goin' to see that you get one. The Cantress gang is plumb busted to flinders. Them that's still left has sure heard the owl hoot, an' they won't be waitin' to hear him again. You saved the bank's money, too—Hell, Fort Smith'll know what you done; an' they'll know who to pass the rewards—'

'I wouldn't touch—'

'Ain't nobody asked you. Half of that money goes to Miz' Bet—'

'Betsy O'Daye?'

'Ain't nothin' wrong with your hearin', is they?'

'Somebody,' I said, 'better look at your head. That girl's the niece of a tickbird an' married to Ed Cantress!'

'Well, Cantress is dead; an' there ain't nothin' wrong with being niece to a tickbird— the ol' coot's done me plenty of favors. Not intentional, mebbe, but he done 'em. As for Betsy O'Daye—how'd you reckon I got them marshals to Ingalls without she passed me on that message you give her?'

'She gave my note straight over to Hanley!'

'When he caught her, she did. She couldn't get out of it. But she give me the gist of it just the same—come clear to Guthrie after me an' give me every blame word of it! If the rights was known—'

But all I could think of right then was finding her. 'Where is she?' I growled; and he

212

kind of grinned a little.

'She *was* at the store—'

That was where I found her.

*   *   *

Been a long time since then. Been a long, long time.

Our kids is grown now and running their own spreads. There ain't a heap left to recall the past. Farms and wire fences have nosed the ranchers out; oil rigs dot the red plains now. My old .44 hangs pegged to the wall, collecting dust like my spurs and saddle. But now and again my mind goes back to the old wild days I used to know—to the wilder nights and the owlhoot trails, to the staccato pound of wind-driven hoofs come churning out of some brush locked draw. Such times I often think of Charlie, and wonder if he's blowing in heaven those tunes he blew so gusty then.